LOVE'S CHRISTMAS BLESSINGS

LAURA V. HILTON

RACHEL J. GOOD

CELEBRATE Lit

First Print November 2018

Celebrate Lit Publishing

www.celebratelitpublishing.com

ISBN: 978-0-9995370-0-8

WINTER'S TREASURE

By Laura V. Hilton

Chapter One

Mackinac County, Michigan

Come to the place of yeast, heat, and treats.

Paris Kauffman trailed a finger over the cramped lettering scratched across the age-old stationary. Who had written it? *Daed*'s tradition to have a treasure hunt as part of her birthday celebration would've been her first guess, but his script looped bold. The handwriting did look somewhat familiar. She stared at it.

"The place of yeast, heat, and treats?" Her best friend, Sarah Fisher, crowded closer to her on the front porch and peered over Paris's shoulder. "It's too early in the *morgen* for puzzles. I haven't had my first cup of *koffee* yet."

Paris shook her head. "It's a treasure hunt." And she hoped this year would yield her greatest treasure, her dream come true, her—

"A *what* hunt?" Sarah frowned.

"Remember I told you how I got my horse last year? *Daed* does a treasure hunt for me every year. Maybe when I figure out all the clues, I'll find a surprise party." And there would be a man there who would only have eyes for her. Someone like… She forced that thought away. *He* was taken. But still, excitement quivered through her. It was Saturday *morgen,* and it'd be so fun to end a day full of adventure and clues with a party. "I've never had one before, and *Daed* said he'd do something special for my twenty-first birthday."

"A surprise party? That'd be lovely." Sarah plucked the note from Paris's gloved hand. "Who would have a birthday treasure hunt for a surprise party? In fact, who would have a birthday treasure hunt? I never heard of such a thing. What would happen if you can't solve the clues?"

"I can solve them." Paris frowned. "Last year they took me all over the farm. Clues were stuck in random places, and I had to go there and find out where to go next. And I had to keep hunting until I found the next clue or the treasure. That's why my horse is named Treasure. And that's why I stopped by your *haus* this *morgen.* My birthday card had a clue that led to you: *A place where a new friendship grows.* You're my newest friend. And you had a note." She flopped the paper between them.

"*Jah.* Your *daed* gave the note to me. With no explanation, except to give it to you. Like he doesn't see you more than I do. Your family is so odd." Sarah rolled her eyes.

That hurt. Every family had their own traditions, didn't they? Paris always thought it was special the way her parents recognized her birthday. As if she was someone important to them, despite the fact that no one else had wanted her. She suppressed that thought with another glance at the cramped handwriting. This wasn't *Daed*'s writing. The clue must've been written by someone else. Where did she know it from?

"So, what are you going to do? If there was a surprise birthday party, I'd know about it. And I haven't heard so much as a whisper." A touch of pique colored Sarah's voice.

"Everyone knows you tell me everything. So, if they wanted it to be a secret they wouldn't tell you." Paris smiled.

"I *can* keep a secret." Sarah huffed. "I never told you—wait, maybe I have. Well, there's…or probably… Hmm. I'm sure there's something I haven't told you."

Paris shook her head. "I'm going to figure out the clues. Do you want to come with me?" She assumed *Daed* had intended her to invite Sarah, because the first clue led to her. But Sarah seemed rather bitter—maybe even angry—today.

An unusual trait for her. Possibly going with Paris would help to lift her spirits.

"I just hope we don't regret this." Sarah sighed. "I'll go tell *Mamm.* Maybe it'll give her hints to do something special for my birthday. She normally just ignores it."

That was sad. Paris would try to do something fun for Sarah's birthday. Maybe the surprise party she wanted. Paris refolded the note with the next address and climbed into the buggy to wait. At least the enclosed vehicle had a heater. Much warmer than Sarah's front porch, with the chilly wind pushing at them. When Sarah returned and sat next to her, Paris turned to her. "What's wrong? I'd thought you'd enjoy going on this adventure with me today."

Sarah tugged her coat closer and hugged herself. "Who else would I want to go on an adventure with? Your adventures are so exciting." Her forced laugh and the attempt at a joke fell flat. She sighed again. "I guess I'm upset because I heard the Stutzmans' grandson, Peter, cannot come and help his grandparents anymore." She swiped her hand across her eyes.

"I'm sorry. You just found out?" She reached for Sarah's hand and squeezed it. Her heart had been broken by a Stutzman, too. Heartbreakers, one and all, apparently. A sympathetic sigh emerged. "I really am sorry." Paris had moped for days when it became clear that Quil Stutzman had chosen another.

"*Jah.* I saw them out by the mailboxes this *morgen* and went to give them a couple loaves of banana bread. They said they got a note from Peter's cousin saying he'll be coming instead."

Peter's cousin? Paris heart lurched, then settled with a sickening thud. Peter had lots of cousins. It didn't necessarily mean it was *him.*

"I thought I was in love with Peter. And I thought he really liked me, too. I mean, we did date the entire time he was here. But he went and married someone else *two weeks* after he returned home. Can you believe it? I was dreaming of his return all fall and now… now…Peter Stutzman broke my heart." She swiped her hand across her eyes. "The Stutzmans' other grandson will have to be super amazing to take Peter's place in my heart."

Paris tried not to scowl. Peter didn't deserve a place in Sarah's heart, if he was a two-timing louse. He had passed out winks to more than just Sarah when he was here. And he wore his handsomeness like an accepted fact. He *knew* he was beyond cute. He must've been courting someone else the entire time he was here if he'd married two weeks after returning home. But who was Paris to judge Sarah for falling for a handsome man. She'd been guilty of that herself. Not with Peter, but another man—Peter's cousin—who was just as heartbreaking.

Sarah brushed at her tears. "Where do you think it is? Yeast, heat, and treats."

Paris handed her the paper. "I think it might be the bakery I worked at this past summer. That kind of reminds me of Naomi's handwriting."

"It could be. I wonder if your *daed* bought you a chocolate-glazed doughnut." Sarah's lips curled. Odd, because Sarah liked the chocolate-glazed ones best. Maybe she was jealous.

If *Daed* intended for Paris to invite Sarah, he would've bought one for her, too. And if he didn't, Paris would get one for her. She wanted to cheer Sarah up. Or at least try.

Paris flicked the reins. Treasure pulled the buggy toward the street.

At the bakery, Naomi smiled when Paris entered. "You figured out my clue. Happy birthday! Go sit at the table by the window. There's another clue waiting there. I'll bring your gift right out to you." She bustled through the swinging door into the back.

Paris giggled and tugged on Sarah's arm heading toward the indicated table, even though none of the other tables in the bakery were in use. Paris had worked there during the summer, and they always closed at ten. People came early for doughnuts and breakfast pastries, and to pick up rolls, bread, and desserts for the day.

She sank into the chair and glanced around the table. Sure enough, in the menu holder was an envelope addressed to Paris Kauffman in someone's neat handwriting. The envelope was a light pink, and the pen a darker pink. A clue there. Who loved pink so much?

It must be…

Paris's hands shook as she pulled out the single sheet of pink paper. Treats you can't beat. It *had* to be—

Movement caught her attention, and she looked up. Naomi approached the table, a small white paper bag in her hand as a bus growled to a stop outside. All three women turned to stare. Unusual, because this town wasn't a regular bus stop. Normally, they had to get a driver to pick them up in another town. A lone Amish man emerged, carrying a big orange bag. He pulled his scarf closer around his face, covering his mouth and nose. Naomi cleared her throat, drawing Paris's attention. "There's one apiece. Sarah's chocolate-glazed doughnut and your favorite apple fritter. I made them to go, because I know you have a bunch of clues to figure out. See you tomorrow. *Nein,* I guess not. It isn't church Sunday. I'll see you later." She set the bag on the table and hurried behind the counter as the sleigh bells hanging on the door rang out a cheery welcome.

Head bent against the wind, the man entered the bakery, looked at the bells, then fished something out of his pocket with his free hand. He pulled out a slip of paper. He glanced toward the girls sitting at the small table, tipped his black hat in cowboy fashion, and nodded. The shadow from his hat concealed his eyes, but he seemed vaguely familiar.

He lowered his scarf and removed his hat.

Blue eyes. Honey blond hair. A square jaw. Handsome. So handsome. Her heart lurched.

Paris caught her breath. *Him.* How could she not have guessed?

Sarah turned. Her mouth formed an O. "Wow. I get first dibs."

She could have him. Because Paris had done everything except handstands and cartwheels to get his attention when she used to live in the lower peninsula, but he couldn't see past the stars in his eyes for another girl.

Aquila Stutzman approached the counter as the bus growled off. He held out the slip of paper to Naomi. "Can you point me in the right direction?"

Naomi fluttered her hand, drawing Paris's attention. "They'll be going that way shortly. I'm sure they won't mind giving you a ride."

He retrieved his paper and turned. Paris started to rise, but Sarah was quicker.

"We're definitely going your way." Sarah snagged the scrap from his loose grip. "Oh, you're the Stutzmans' grandson coming to help out? We're practically neighbors." She batted her eyelashes.

Paris looked away. The Stutzmans had *two* super-amazing grandsons—except Paris had once considered him the best. And Sarah was smitten. Again.

Of course, so was Paris. But she wasn't quite as bold as her friend. And this man had a girl he was courting back home, just like Peter did. No way would Paris get involved with another two-timing Stutzman.

Maybe she should warn Sarah to guard her heart this time. Tell her about Priscilla Graber and how Quil had courted her off and on since he was sixteen.

Unless...Unless, as in her secret dreams and deepest wishes he remembered Paris and had come here to find her. To woo her. To—

"Aquila Stutzman," the man said, his gaze scanning Sarah and Paris. "My friends call me Quil."

No flash of recognition lit his eyes.

And Paris's heart folded in on itself.

❄

"Quil," the girl with strawberry-blonde hair gushed, a welcoming smile filling her face. "I'm Sarah." Her lashes fluttered so rapidly he wondered if she had something in her eyes.

Her dark-haired friend stood quietly behind her. Not smiling, not blinking, and not gushing. Just looking at him as if he'd fallen from Mars instead of simply getting off the bus. She had brown eyes. Dark lashes. And a splattering of freckles across her cheeks.

Beautiful, despite the white scar under her bottom lip. And she looked vaguely familiar. He was pretty sure he knew her from somewhere. Though if he did, he couldn't think how, or where, or even who she might be.

"Nice to meet you, Sarah." Quil dragged his eyes away from the girl who'd snagged his attention long enough to glance at the strawberry blonde, then his gaze locked on the darker-haired girl again. He took a step forward. "And you are?"

"Paris Kauffman," she said quietly.

Paris Kauffman. He'd known someone named Paris once. Years ago, before his grandparents lived in Michigan's Upper Peninsula, they'd lived in the larger community in the Lower Peninsula. Except her last name hadn't been Kauffman, or had it? He narrowed his eyes, trying to recall the girl who'd sat a couple rows ahead of him on the girls' side of the school. She'd been an *Englisch* child in the foster system and hadn't known the dialect the Amish used. She'd struggled to learn their language as surely as he'd struggled to learn *Englisch.* Her foster parents must've adopted her. If this was the same girl. Woman. "Have you ever lived near Mio?"

Her eyes widened, a hint of a smile reaching them now. And maybe hope. "*Jah,* until about two years ago."

He should've known her as a young woman then, should've seen her at singings and frolics. He studied her, frowning, and tried to remember. Something niggled but stayed out of his grasp.

The baker bustled up, clutching another white bag. "Here you go. It's Paris's birthday, and her *daed* said to give a doughnut to her and everyone with her. Her favorite is apple fritters, so that's what you're getting, if it's okay. Hope you like it."

"I do. *Danki.*" He turned back to Paris. "Happy birthday."

Sarah scowled a little and moved slightly nearer to him. "Her parents are sending her on a scavenger hunt for her birthday. Have you ever heard of such a silly thing?"

"Treasure hunt." Paris raised her chin slightly as if daring him to make a big deal out of it.

He wouldn't dream of it. Instead, he motioned toward the envelope in her hand as he glanced at Sarah. "Unusual, maybe. But sweet." He looked to Paris. "Where to next?"

Paris didn't consult the pink sheet of paper. Instead, she pointed to the right. "I'm pretty sure its two doors down. The candy shop." A small smile curved her lips.

"Let's go then." He reached for the other white paper bag, similar to his, on the table, strode across the room, then opened the door wide. "After you." He plopped his hat back on his head

"*Danki,* Quil." Sarah smiled coyly.

"*Jah, danki.*" Paris followed her friend out the door. "You can put your bag and the doughnuts in my buggy. I'm going there." She pointed toward a pink sign that read Sweet Treats, then continued down the sidewalk. Sarah stayed behind to walk with him.

"Tell me about yourself, Quil," Sarah cooed.

He glanced at a beat-up pickup that pulled into one of the

parking places along the curb. Right behind the lone buggy. "Nothing to tell." He opened the door and tossed his bag into the backseat.

"Brothers, sisters, girlfriend..." Sarah prodded as he set the bags of doughnuts on the front seat.

"*Jah.*" Quil let that comment answer for all three, even though the last one wasn't true. Not anymore. He pressed his lips together. A muscle jumped in his jaw as he fought to keep the pain at bay. *Jah,* he'd had a girlfriend. But she hadn't turned out to be the girl he thought she was. Instead, she'd eloped with his cousin Peter. Because they'd both been baptized, they were in danger of the bann if they didn't kneel and confess. They would, sooner rather than later, because Peter's job depended upon him being a church member in *gut* standing.

Enough of Sarah's invasive questions. He hurried to catch up with Paris. He liked her quiet gentleness and the way she didn't chase him.

The bells jingled on the candy shop door as Paris yanked it open. A woman emerged from the back, squealed, and rushed out to engulf Paris in a hug. "Happy birthday! Your *daed* said to get you a half pound of any kind of fudge you want."

"*Danki,* Agnes." Paris returned her hug and headed toward the glass case as Quil stumbled to a stop, inhaling the rich, tantalizingly sweet smells of the confections. This would be a place to stay away from, but oh, it smelled so *gut.*

"I don't know how I'll ever choose." Paris leaned over the display, almost pressing her nose against it. So sweet. Innocent, like a small child. He smiled.

Sarah lingered beside Quil. "Don't you want to see? Maybe choose some candy?" There was a broad hint in her voice, as if she wanted him to buy candy for her. So not happening. And with *grossdaadi*'s recent diagnosis of diabetes, he wouldn't tempt his grandparents by bringing anything from this particular shop into the *haus.* Still, his mouth watered, and against his will, he marched toward the display and stopped next to Paris. A hint of vanilla teased his sense of smell. Her or the candy? He sure wasn't about to lean closer to her and sniff to find out.

Paris pointed toward something chocolatey. "I'll take some of that one, I think." She glanced up at Quil. "You aren't allergic to nuts, are you?"

"*Nein,* but it isn't for me. It's your birthday." His voice came out huskier than he liked.

"I'm going to share, of course. I can't eat all this by myself. I'd be so chubby I wouldn't fit through the door."

"Fudge has no calories on your birthday." Agnes lifted the blade she held and wagged it at her. *Gut* thing she was behind the counter and a glass case separated them. "Besides, you are in no danger of getting fat."

"*Danki* for sharing." Quil's eyes were drawn to her curves. Agnes was right. He jerked his gaze away. Uncomfortable with the direction of the conversation, Quil stepped away from the area teeming with temptation and walked over to the window. A sticker was plastered to the upper corner, marking it as new, maybe recently installed. A cardboard leaning against the pane read "Closed." The side seen from the street must read "Open", but he hadn't noticed. He'd been too focused on keeping his distance from Sarah and catching up with Paris.

His gaze shot to her again. If she moved up here two years ago, he must've had some interaction with her, church or something, since he left school at fourteen. He furrowed his brow. Unless she was adept at being a wallflower, he couldn't remember her past their school days.

Of course, that'd been when Priscilla had moved to Mio, and he'd only had eyes for her. Thought she was *Gott*'s will, because the biblical Aquila's spouse had been named Priscilla.

Another pang stabbed his heart.

Agnes boxed Paris's selection of fudge and handed it to her

with another letter. Sarah leaned close to Paris as she opened it. "One man's trash is another man's treasure," Paris read out loud.

Quil frowned.

She snapped her fingers. "I bet it's the salvage grocery store."

"I did say it's a scavenger hunt, right?" Sarah's smile was a bit condescending. "Hope you don't mind getting to your grandparents' place late, Quil."

"They, ah, aren't expecting me quite yet. I came early." To get away from Peter and his new bride, once the girl of Quil's dreams. But as his gaze rested on Paris, the memory somehow wasn't quite so painful.

❄

Paris wasn't sure where to start at the salvage grocery store. She hesitated at the doorway, looking around. It was Amish owned and operated, but she didn't think they'd have a note for her or a gift. Then again, they had to have some clue for her to follow, or she wouldn't have been sent here.

Quil brushed past her. "I need to pick something up. I'll be right back." He hurried off, Sarah two steps behind. An *Englisch* clerk stopped straightening the shelves and followed them.

It wouldn't be long before Quil and Sarah were a couple. Paris sighed. Because Quil had never noticed her as a child, tween, or teen, she had no reason to expect he would now, even if he was available. Which he wasn't, because he'd answered Sarah with an all-inclusive *jah*. He always seemed to look right through her, over her, or around her. It'd been a relief to move away from Mio, knowing she'd never see him again. And it'd been shocking when his grandparents moved up to the new community, having bought a Christmas tree farm after the previous owners decided not to return to the area. Even worse when Peter followed, though if he ever mentioned his cousin Quil, she never heard.

Amish didn't even decorate with trees for Christmas. But Bishop Nehemiah Brunstetter—better known as Bishop Miah—had approved the purchase because it'd generate income for the Stutzmans. And because they'd previously owned a tree farm. He was rumored to be more lenient than some, but also more orthodox in his scriptural beliefs. She didn't have enough experience to decide whether the rumor was true or not. But he was nice.

The *Englisch* clerk approached her, her gaze skimming over Paris's clothing. When had they hired her? Her name tag read Meredith. She smoothed her hands over her blue jeans, then smiled, too brightly. "Are you Paris? I asked that other girl." She jerked her hand over her shoulder.

"I'm Paris."

Meredith's smile softened. "The manager has something for you back in his office. You know where it is?"

Paris nodded. "Thank you." She headed toward the back of the store and the flapping doors that led into the recesses.

Gideon looked up from his messy desk as Paris approached. He reached for a basket filled with pink tissue paper and wrapped with pink plastic wrap that was perched on a high stack of folders. The folders slid in two different directions as he moved it, and he mumbled something Paris couldn't hear. With one hand he pushed the basket toward her, dislodging more papers and files, and with his other, he grabbed for the files tumbling off the desk.

She started around the desk to help, but he waved her away. "Take it and go. Happy birthday."

"Thank you." Paris took the basket and left his office, somewhat put off by his unusual brusqueness. She wandered the perimeter of the store, glancing down each aisle for Sarah and Quil, but didn't see them anywhere. Finally, she took a Cherry Coke from the refrigerator case, because she really should buy something, and went to the cash register. Meredith eyed the pink-wrapped basket, as if checking to see if it'd been opened, took the money for the drink, and nodded toward the door. "Your friends are waiting outside."

Maybe she should've bought them a drink, too. Paris reached for her wallet again. "I'll take two more drinks."

Meredith's face wore a hint of a smirk. "You needn't bother. Your friend bought two and gave one to him. He's new in town, isn't he?" The smirk turned into a dreamy smile.

Paris fought to keep a scowl under control. Another boy-crazy woman, just like Sarah. But she'd been just like them—until she wised up.

"Just arrived today." And he'd already disrupted her life. Again. Still.

She really needed to warn Sarah to keep her distance. Because Quil was a two-timer, just like his cousin.

A heartbreaker.

In more ways than one.

Chapter Two

Quil should've walked. He should've refused a ride from Paris and walked. Not only would he have gotten to his grandparents' *haus* faster, but he also would've escaped Sarah's clutches.

He wasn't interested.

At least, not in Sarah.

But he hadn't exactly told her "no." Instead, he'd gratefully accepted the drink, even though it was chilled on an already frigid day. He'd taken his purchases and gone outside to wait in the buggy. Though now that he'd bought the gifts for Paris's birthday, he second-guessed the wisdom of them.

Quil stopped short of entering the buggy. Sarah had followed him out, and no way was he going to be alone with her in the confines of a closed vehicle. Not even if it had a heater. That would be a recipe for disaster.

He reached into the backseat and tucked the plastic bag from the store into his orange tote, zipped it shut, and leaned against the buggy, sipping his root beer. Might as well freeze his insides, too. He wasn't used to such cold winds in his area of Mio, Michigan.

"How long are you here? Permanently, I hope?" Sarah's

eyelashes were set on auto-flutter. Disturbing. And distracting. She tugged on her scarf, wrapping it more securely around her neck.

He sighed. How should he answer? He'd come to help with the Christmas tree sales, cutting, bundling, shipping, and assisting the individual local buyers who came by the farm to cut trees for themselves. He eyed Sarah. He intended to stay—or had intended to stay. Probably not the wisest decision, but his grandparents were getting up there in age and needed someone to manage the farm. In fact, that'd been their sole purpose in buying land here after their sons—Quil's *daed* and *onkels*—took over the old tree farm. There wasn't enough land to support another generation of young men looking to start families. And not a lot of real estate for sale. At least not at present. They'd intended Peter to take it over. Quil was next in line.

Some of the young men had decided they'd eventually join the Upper Peninsula community, providing it rebounded after the bad wildfire. Peter hadn't sounded very positive when he'd returned to woo Priscilla away from Quil. To distance himself from his broken heart, and the newlyweds Quil decided to come early and check it out for himself. And from first glance, it seemed to be growing. It now boasted a bakery, a candy shop, and a salvage grocery store that housed a small post office. All three appeared new.

"Aren't you going to answer me?" Sarah's brows drew down. Her lips were hidden behind the scarf, but judging by her eyes, he guessed she pouted.

What had she asked him? He frowned, trying to remember. Oh, if he planned to stay. Permanently. He lifted a shoulder. "That remains to be seen." Though, if he left here, where would he go? Home, to see Peter and Priscilla happily growing their family? Or maybe he could go farther west to the Amish community in Montana. He could at least check it out by going hunting there during the appropriate seasons.

Her eyes brightened. "You've given me hope. Paris might be having a surprise birthday party today. She thinks she is, anyway. If she does, you can take me home afterwards."

Wow. He'd never met such a forward girl and didn't appreciate it. He drained his bottle and tossed it into the nearby trash receptacle. "Guys like to do the chasing."

Sarah's brow furrowed. "Okay, then. You can chase me." She turned just a tiny bit, as if she intended to dash off. As if she thought he'd intended a literal game of tag.

It was a pure blessing straight from *Gott* when Paris exited the building, carrying a pink-wrapped wicker basket and a bottle of pop. Singular. Because Sarah hadn't treated her as she had him. Guilt washed through him. He should've thought of her. But at least she had a drink.

Paris's gaze darted from him to Sarah, then to the drink in Sarah's hand before her smile appeared. It seemed dimmer than before.

Quil stepped away from the buggy. "I should've thought to get you a drink." Cherry Coke. He'd remember that.

Her forehead wrinkled. "Why would you?"

Ouch. "Old friends?" He hitched an eyebrow. They might've been friends in Mio. And if not, he always had plenty of friends, so what's a few more?

Paris's brows rose in response. "As I recall, we weren't friends."

"You wound me. We went to school together. I think we even had key parts in the Christmas play when we were thirteen."

Her eyes flashed as if he'd said something unkind. "You think."

Was he wrong? Maybe he'd better write home and ask his sister if she remembered Paris Kauffman.

Sarah sidled close, making it plain she didn't like his attention on Paris. "Obviously, you aren't friends." Her smile said it was a *gut* thing.

We aren't friends, yet. Why was Sarah even along for the ride if she wasn't a *gut* friend to sweet, kind Paris? What could he do to improve her birthday? Time to change the subject. Quil nodded at the basket in Paris's hand. "Is there a note in there?"

She blew out a breath and opened the buggy door. "Let's find out."

Quil hurried to untie the horse, then clambered into the backseat. He moved his orange bag onto the seat beside him, so Sarah wouldn't crawl in back with him.

"Because the bakery is closing for the day, let's go back to the candy shop, eat our doughnuts, and if you want, you can have a cup of *koffee.* Agnes gives away free *koffee* to customers because her candy is so expensive. We can open the basket there," Paris said.

Quil's stomach rumbled in response. He loved apple fritters, too. Especially with a mug of hot apple cider. But a cup of *koffee* would work in a pinch. Either way it'd warm what the icy drink had chilled.

"Would you rather I take you home first?" Paris twisted to look at him. "I don't want your grandparents to worry."

"They don't know I'm coming." Well, they did, but they didn't expect him so soon. "*Nein,* I'll keep my eye on you, Little Miss Birthday Girl."

"Your eye on me? What do you think Little Miss Birthday Girl will do? Seduce you?" Her cheeks flared red.

Sarah gasped.

The temperature rose about fifty degrees in the buggy. The air charged, and he sucked in a breath. He hadn't expected that comeback. Not from her. Her friend, maybe. He didn't venture a glance toward Sarah. Instead, he maintained eye contact with Paris. He'd play along. "You never know. I am quite the catch." He blew on his glove-covered fingertips before brushing them against his shirt.

Paris snorted. "I don't know if you're still a catch or not. But you smell like fried chicken."

Sarah gasped again.

Quil glanced down at his clothes, checking for chicken crumbs or greasy spots from his unconventional breakfast. He didn't see anything potentially embarrassing. He took a deep breath, then chuckled. A brief, puff-of-air chuckle. "Is that right?"

❄

Paris quickly twisted away and released the brakes. She hadn't meant to say that, hadn't intended to flirt with him, and hadn't planned to let him know about her long-term crush. But perhaps he wouldn't understand the underlying currents. And hopefully her chatty, flirty friend would fill in the silence before he had a chance to dissect her comments.

Still a catch. Her face burned hotter. Even worse, she'd said *seduce.*

Sarah stared at her in horror, her mouth agape. For once, silent.

Shame filled Paris, and she slumped in the seat. If word about this got out—and it would, she cut a glance toward Sarah—then she'd be in serious trouble, because she'd used a word like "seduce" with a man. That mild flirting about him being a catch might be excused, but their orthodox bishop would have reason to question the purity of her thoughts. Not to mention her parents' reaction. She didn't know how to fix it.

Especially when a spark of interest had flashed in Quil's eyes. She'd finally gotten his attention, but in the worst possible way.

"How'd you know what I ate on the bus ride?" Confusion filled his voice.

"For breakfast?" Sarah regained her voice.

Paris breathed a sigh of relief. The conversation could be centered on food. Far better than her stupid comment.

"*Jah,* actually. I left home yesterday, but the bridge was closed for hours. So, I saved a piece and ate it cold." He cleared his throat. "A cup of *koffee* sounds *sur gut.*"

Paris glanced toward the basket on the seat beside her. She

couldn't think what *Mamm* would've put in there, but she couldn't wait to find out. Hopefully, it wouldn't be anything potentially embarrassing. Like fried chicken for a picnic lunch to share with her friends, no, companions. She'd already humiliated herself enough today.

She glanced in the rearview mirror but focused on the man in the backseat.

Although, other than the initial shock, Quil's expression had settled. A twinkle appeared in his eyes, a dimple flashed, and his lips twitched as if he'd been tempted to do more than chuckle.

Paris drove the buggy to Main Street, parked in front of Agnes's candy shop, and jumped out. Sarah hung back, waiting, even though she was quite capable of getting out on her own.

An internal war broke out in Paris. She wanted Quil to herself, but she was glad for the barrier as she tried to regain her composure and emotional distance.

The slight smile on his face faded, twisting into something that might've been a scowl, but if it was, it quickly disappeared. He clambered out and held out his hand to Sarah, who emerged as if she were some fine lady in those regency romance novels Sarah liked to read. At least the gloved hands made it seem that way, though Paris doubted the heroines in those books wore thick winter gloves when they went out on the town.

Paris gathered her basket along with the two white bags from the bakery and went up the stairs to the sidewalk. Quil hurried behind her, then reached around her to open the door. He held it wide and waved his free hand with a flourish. "Paris." His voice was low and rumbly and sent a shiver down her spine.

Something clattered in the kitchen, followed by a cry of pain, drowning out any further words he might've said—like Sarah's name. It was better Paris didn't know.

She dropped the basket and bags on the nearest table—a small one, for two—and dashed through the swinging half-door to the back.

Agnes clutched her reddening hand. A pot holder lay on the floor next to a kettle that'd spilled melted chocolate on the tiles. The mess spread toward the two women.

"What happened?" Paris snatched up the potholder before the chocolate reached it. It was wet, which would cause it to transmit heat, allowing Agnes to get burnt.

Agnes made a sound that resembled a sob. "Stupid mistake. My mind was on something else. I should've known better." She shook her head and grabbed a rag. "What can I help you with?" Her smile was forced. Strained. Was it because her hand hurt? If only there was some way to help.

"*Nix.* We just stopped to eat our doughnuts and get a cup of *koffee,* but I'll help you clean this up first. And if you need to talk about something, I can listen."

"I've got it. You go have fun." Agnes dropped the rag on the mess and picked up a blue plastic pail.

"If it's a bad time..." Paris glanced around for some sort of cleaning fluid but didn't see any.

"It's not. Help yourself to *koffee.* Cups are over there." She pointed toward a metal tree on the counter. Her gaze shot to something over Paris's shoulder. Her face colored. "Customers aren't allowed back here."

Since when? Agnes had never objected before. Paris glanced over her shoulder. Quil stood in the doorway, his eyes wide. He backed out, letting the door swing shut.

"Are you sure you don't want help?" Paris hesitated.

Agnes lifted three cups off the rack. "You know where the *koffee* is. I just made some fresh. Go on now. Get to know that young man and have fun."

"That young man" was the bane of Paris's existence. She sighed, forced a smile, and took two of the offered mugs. *"Danki.* I don't want *koffee,* though." She wrinkled her nose.

Agnes laughed. "I forgot. You and your aversion to *koffee.*"

Paris grinned and pushed through the swinging door.

Quil and Sarah sat opposite one another at a larger table. They'd stripped off their outerwear, leaving their coats on the fourth chair. Sarah had already gotten out the doughnuts and served them on individual napkins.

The only empty chair was between Sarah and Quil. Sarah probably wanted a full face-view of the hunky man. Unfortunately, that meant Paris had to breathe in the smell of fried chicken. A food she normally liked, but it didn't work as cologne. Especially when mixed with another fresher scent, like he'd been rolling around in pine needles. She loved the piney scent. Was that cologne? Not many Amish men wore cologne. Just the single, unbaptized ones who wanted to bend the rules. Maybe soap? Or was it natural, because his family owned a tree farm?

The seating arrangement would be even worse if Sarah decided to play footsie under the table.

Paris cringed.

"Are you okay?" Quil peered at her, then took the two still-empty mugs dangling by their handles from her fingers. "Only two? Can I help with the *koffee?*"

"Feel free. I don't like *koffee.*" Paris pointed him toward the *koffee* pot, then took off her black bonnet, gloves, coat, and scarf. She dropped them on the chair already in use as a catch-all and sat in the chair Quil vacated.

"Remember, I have first dibs," Sarah hissed.

Paris nodded. It was better for Sarah to be next to him than across from him. At least the way Paris saw it. That way they could make eyes at each other, and she'd be out of the way and not have to watch it.

A few minutes later, Quil returned with the filled mugs. He set them down and reached for a couple of sugar packets from a bowl in the center of the table. He shook them as he sat, then ripped them open. Sarah reached for the hazelnut-flavored creamer from another bowl beside the sugar.

"So, Quil. You never answered me. Brothers, sisters, girlfriend?"

He shifted uncomfortably. "I did answer. I said *jah.* I have brothers, sisters, and, I mean, but…" He coughed. Choked, really. Then downed half the mug of *koffee.* Without the sugar. He still held the opened packets in his other hand.

But that was answer enough for Paris.

Two-timing jerk. She kicked Sarah under the table and mouthed, "Beware."

❄

Quil winced as a tennis shoe connected with his calf. He also caught the silent warning Paris sent her friend, "Beware." Great, if Sarah listened, but he feared she wouldn't. Besides, what could he say? If he confessed to his recent demotion to "ex" status, she'd be unstoppable. But if he lied and said he was taken, then the intriguing Paris would definitely be off-limits.

And he didn't want her to be.

Then again, if she was from Mio, she already knew about Priscilla—

The shoe slammed into his shin again, harder this time. "Ow!"

Paris gasped and glanced down as if she wanted to make a quick getaway or hide under the table. Not that it'd be much of a hiding place.

Part of him admired her spunk at trying to get her friend's behavior in line. She was an intriguing girl who seemed sweet but could pack quite a kick. In addition to snapping out sassy comebacks. He wanted to find out more about her.

Sarah looked puzzled and stared at him. "Are you okay?"

Time to deflect, redirect, or something. Quil put his mug down and nudged the basket toward Paris. "Open up, Little Miss Birthday Girl. I want to see what you got."

Then he dumped the sugar into his remaining *koffee,* took a bite of doughnut, and went to refill his mug.

He'd be on a sugar high by the time he got to *grossmammi*'s *haus* and in danger of being in the throes of a major crush.

On Paris.

Chapter Three

Paris slid the basket a little closer as Quil lowered himself back into the chair. With an embarrassed smile, she undid the pink plastic wrap twisted shut over the basket. The contents were hidden with pink and white tissue paper. She pulled the paper aside and removed a small box containing hot chocolate sticks in three different flavors: dark chocolate, milk chocolate, and white chocolate with vanilla. Oh, they looked so *gut.*

"*Jah,* please." Sarah reached across the table to snag one, but Paris swatted her hand away.

"I'll share later. Maybe." It might improve Sarah's attitude. On the other hand, Sarah's obvious boy-chasing was annoying, especially because earlier today she'd claimed to have a broken heart and would "never get over Peter." Quil chuckled again.

"Meanie." Sarah sulked, her lower lip protruding.

Paris pulled out a case of assorted sewing scissors with pink handles, a metal thimble, and another note. She couldn't wait to use these tools to make herself a new dress.

Quil downed his *koffee* again. "I'm sorry. I was thoughtless to not ask earlier. Can I get you something else to drink?

She shook her head. "*Nein, danki.*"

He frowned. "You sure?"

"Positive. I still have my unopened Cherry Coke in the buggy." Paris ripped open the envelope.

"Should I get your pop for you, then? It'll freeze if left out there." He stood.

"It'll wait." She pulled the paper out of the envelope. "A place, not home, where love abides."

Silence.

Sarah shook her head. "Where could your *daed* mean?"

Paris shrugged. "This is a tough one. Any suggestions?"

Quil frowned, reached into his pocket and pulled out the slip of paper with an address on it that he'd shown Naomi. Quil glanced at it, then slid it closer to Paris. "*Mammi* always said that about her home. Looks like our next stop might be my grandparents' *haus*." He refilled his *koffee* and settled back into the chair.

Paris glanced at it a second before Sarah reached across and snagged the note.

"Oh, we'll be going right past my *haus*, Quil, so you'll know where I live. I expect we'll see a lot of each other," Sarah said. "I told you we're practically neighbors."

Quil shifted. Squirmed.

Paris almost felt sorry for him.

He ripped open two more packets of sugar, dumped them in, and glanced at her. "Do you live near there, too?"

"About a mile away. You won't see me very often, except for frolics and church Sundays." She picked up her apple fritter. "Guess we'll enjoy this, then get you home sooner rather than later."

"I don't mind hanging out with you…uh, both." Quil caught her gaze.

Paris's face heated because Quil had focused his attention on her. And because she was slightly embarrassed for Sarah that her friend's attention had pushed him away. She dipped her head, trying not to look at Sarah.

Agnes came through the swinging half-door, carrying a small plate. "Do you all mind trying this? It's a new recipe and is supposed to be dipped in chocolate, but…" She half-laughed.

Quil reached for a piece first and examined it. "Is it fudge?"

"Fudge bites."

He took a bite. "It's *sur gut.* Tastes like coconut and some type of nut." He tilted his head. "It'll be *gut* dipped in chocolate."

"You're my new favorite person. Come back anytime you want to taste test." Agnes beamed. "It's mashed potatoes, coconut, and almonds."

Sarah wrinkled her nose. "Ew, Agnes. I wouldn't tell customers they have potatoes in them. I'll pass. Besides, I'm allergic to peanuts, and I'm not sure if that would include almonds or not. I'd rather not take any chances."

"You better not have eaten any of that peanut butter fudge you bought yesterday then," Agnes said dryly.

Paris tried to smother a giggle, but Quil snorted.

Sarah huffed.

"Are you brave enough to try it, Paris?" Agnes's lips twitched.

"Sure." Paris took a piece and nibbled it. "You can't taste the potatoes at all. It's kind of like the filling in a certain candy bar. Really *gut.*"

"You should try to make chocolate and cherry fudge sometime." Quil took the third piece that'd been intended for Sarah. "Because cherries are grown in Michigan."

"That does sound *gut.*" Agnes tilted her head as if she were considering it. "I do make a chocolate-covered cherry recipe. I could come up with something, I'm sure." She stepped backwards. "I need to get back to work. You have fun now. Happy birthday again, Paris."

Sarah rolled her eyes as Agnes returned behind the counter. "I wonder if your *daed* realized how this would appear with you going around collecting gifts and wishes. It's filling your head with self-importance and pride. Someone's going to complain to the bishop about this. You know it's a sin to flaunt yourself, Paris."

And that someone would likely be Paris's former best friend. Sarah truly must be miserable today to treat her this way. Although, it wasn't the first time. She did have a lot of moody spells. And if her family didn't celebrate her birthday she could understand and accept jealousy.

Paris swallowed the bite of apple fritter "It's *gut* I have you to keep me fully grounded then."

"I think it's fine to have one day to enjoy your birthday," Quil said quietly. "My family has a birthday week."

"*Jah,* but this elaborate? My parents don't do anything for my birthday, except a cupcake and a new dress or something *useful.*" She punctuated it with a glare at Paris.

Quil shrugged and leaned back in his chair. "Sounds like sour grapes to me, Sarah. Jealousy is a sin. I think this is sweet and shows how much her parents love her."

Wow. His words warmed Paris inside and out. She never thought he'd defend her.

"But to involve the whole community?" Sarah twisted to stare at him. "That's just wrong."

Paris sighed and finished off her doughnut. Her stomach hurt, but not from the treat. She blinked the burn from her eyes. This Quil would be easy to fall for, but she couldn't trust him. And how could her friend turn on her so easily? She shouldn't have invited her along. "I'll take you home, too, Sarah." She pulled a napkin from the dispenser and wiped her fingers with it.

"Just leave me off at the Stutzmans'. I'll show Quil around the neighborhood." Sarah's eyes brightened with her smile, and she bounced off the seat. Her *koffee* sloshed, spilling on the table. "Let's go."

"Showing Quil around will be sweet of you, Sarah." Paris smiled. "He'll appreciate it. Great idea."

"I know." Sarah giggled. "I'll take him on the grand tour."

Plus, it'd open the door wide for Sarah and Quil to start dating. That would cheer Sarah up and she'd be kind…er.

Jah, as much as it hurt, stepping away would be the nice thing to do.

Quil opened his mouth, shut it, and grabbed a wad of napkins. He cleaned up Sarah's mess and dropped the tissues into the trashcan by the door.

Paris bundled up in her outerwear, yelled good-bye to Agnes, grabbed her basket, and headed toward the door.

Quil grabbed his coat and shoved his arms into the sleeves as he hurried after her.

"Wait for me." Sarah crashed into the table. It scraped across the floor, and probably spilled more *koffee.*

Paris ignored her. She pulled her scarf tighter around her neck as she rushed down the steps to the street.

Quil's hand closed over her shoulder as she slid the basket into the buggy. Shock waves coursed through her body.

His hand trembled, and he cleared his throat. "Look. I think it's sweet what your *daed* is doing. And…and Priscilla and I are no longer together. She married my cousin."

Paris twisted around, dislodging his hand. He stood close. Too close. And he made no effort to back away.

❄

Quil couldn't say why he needed her to know that. Or maybe he could. Even though he might not have noticed Paris Kauffman in Mio, he was aware of her now. He glanced at his hand. Had she noticed the sparks between them?

Her eyes narrowed. "*Jah,* and you're looking for a temporary fling just like your cousin, ain't so? You won't be finding it here."

Ouch. Words of denial sprang to his lips, but he bit them back. She was feisty. He had to admire that. Actually, he respected a lot about her. How had Priscilla ever swayed him away from this girl…if she was the same Paris he'd known?

But the answer to that was obvious. Priscilla was beautiful, generously endowed, and his male hormones had taken over. His, and every other single male in Mio. It'd been beyond *wunderbaar* when she'd noticed him. And terrifying that he'd lose her, especially because rumor had it that she'd stepped out on him. He'd been afraid to confront her about it.

He should've found the courage, because he could've walked away before he'd gotten hurt.

He gulped down a lump that formed in his throat and stared at Paris. Not quite as beautiful as Priscilla, but intriguing. He wanted to go out with her. Get to know her.

"Quil, why didn't you wait? I need help down the stairs." Sarah broke into his thoughts.

A fake smile twisted Paris's lips. "There's your fling. Count me out."

He forced that stubborn lump down again and bit back more words. It'd be better to show her his interest than to attempt to argue its existence.

He swung around and held out his hand to Sarah. The steps were still snow-covered. He supposed she might be worried about falling, especially because she wore shoes with little or no tread.

She gripped his hand with a surprising strength. One that almost seemed possessive. Her lips were pressed together, eyes hard, as she glared past him at Paris.

That persistent lump fought for control of his throat.

Sarah knew or at least sensed his interest lay with Paris and not with her. And she seemed determined not to lose.

He couldn't let her win.

Besides, he needed to be sure of his own emotions, not fall into another relationship on the rebound.

He pulled his hand from Sarah's grip, dipping his head as she went past him to the buggy. He pulled in a deep breath and exhaled it on a prayer. *Lord, guide my paths. Make them straight and clear.*

Because they were very murky right now.

❄

Paris pulled up in the Stutzmans' drive, a mild throbbing behind her eyes. Sarah had sat beside her in the front but swiveled around to see Quil. She kept up constant chatter on the way there, talking about herself and her family, telling him everything he'd ever need to know about her.

Whatever happened to the thrill of discovery?

He'd remained quiet, except for an occasional grunt in reply to something Sarah had said. Had he told the truth about not being interested in a fling with Sarah? Or had she made him mad by calling his bluff?

Time would tell.

Paris got out of the buggy, tethered the horse, then followed Quil and Sarah to the house.

Quil's *grossmammi* dashed out and wrapped him in a hug. "Look at you. When did you get here?"

"The bus dropped me off in town. Paris gave me a ride out because she was coming this way."

"I wish I would've known you were coming. I would've fixed something special for dinner. As it is, we're just having meatloaf, scalloped potatoes, and green beans."

Quil grinned. "I love your meatloaf. We'll have enough left over for sandwiches, right?"

"But of course." His *grossmammi* Phoebe looked over her shoulder, nodded at Sarah, who she'd talked to just that morning. Who probably knew about Peter's interest in her and would tattle to Quil about it later. Or who might even have suspected Sarah was stalking the mailboxes so she could "accidentally" run into them and ask about Peter.

After a moment, she fixed her gaze on Paris. "Paris, *schatz,* I have something for you. Come in. Quil, tell your *grossdaadi* to come in from the barn, and we'll have some pie."

Paris almost groaned. If she'd known pie would be served, she wouldn't have eaten the doughnut. But maybe she could take hers to go, because she'd be following the rest of the clues solo.

She followed Quil's *grossmammi* inside, painfully aware Sarah had trailed after him to the barn.

"Your *mamm* asked me to make you a dress because she couldn't do it without your knowing. I hope you like the color." She led the way into the living room and picked up some folded material the color of the sky.

The color of Quil's eyes.

Too bad she had to notice that.

"It's beautiful, Phoebe. *Danki.*" It was a finished dress, but she'd try it on far away from Sarah so she wouldn't have to listen to any more digs.

"Your *daed* gave me a letter, too. Now, what did I do with it?" She glanced around. "Quil's arrival has me all in a dither. I did write and invite him, of course, when Peter proved himself unworthy of this farm. Foolish *bu* wasting his chances." She scoffed. "I have high hopes for Quil. He always—well, usually—was the one with a head on his shoulders. At least until that Priscilla entered the picture. Such foolishness, believing that she was his soulmate because the biblical Aquila had a bride by that name." She shook her head. "So glad to know he moved on, but unfortunately, Peter fell for her wiles and got caught in the snare."

What? Paris frowned. Quil really wasn't with Priscilla anymore?

"Such sadness, Peter running off with that woman and eloping. My heart is broken. But maybe Quil will learn *Mammi* Phoebe knows best. I've told him for years he can't see the tree for the forest."

Paris nodded as if she knew what Phoebe was talking about,

but she really didn't have the vaguest idea. Besides, wasn't the cliché he couldn't see the forest for the trees?

The kitchen door opened and shut. Then a chair slid across the wooden floor.

Phoebe glanced toward the kitchen. "The men are in. Let's have a slice of pie while I try to remember what I did with the letter. I'm sure I put it someplace where I wouldn't lose it."

Paris impulsively reached out and pulled Phoebe into a hug. "Danki for the dress. I love the color."

Phoebe returned the hug. "Bless you, dear child. I hope this birthday is beyond your wildest dreams. And it's *wunderbaar* Quil arrived in time for it. I never thought he would. Now he'll be able to… well, I better say no more. Come now. Let's not keep them waiting." Phoebe pulled away and went into the kitchen.

Her husband John had already poured four cups of *koffee* and set them on the table. "Water, as usual, Paris?" He glanced at her when she came into the room.

"*Jah, danki.* That'd be great."

Quil stood and pulled out the chair next to him. "Sit here, Paris."

Paris glanced around the room. "Where's Sarah?"

John set the glass of water on the table. "She had to, uh, well, she'll be right back."

Paris hung her coat on the hook and pulled off her gloves and her bonnet, stuffing them into a coat pocket. She turned to find Phoebe standing close to her.

Phoebe pulled her into her arms again. "Call me *Mammi* Phoebe," she whispered. "Now go and make my dreams come true."

Chapter Four

Quil stood behind the empty chair, hoping Paris would sit there before Sarah came out of the bathroom. He didn't understand the antagonism between Paris and Sarah, and he hated that Sarah seemed to have latched onto him. He didn't know how to stop her, short of bluntly stating he wasn't interested, and that seemed cruel.

Something resembling fear crossed Paris's expression as she stepped out of *Mammi*'s hug. She glanced at Quil, her eyes wide, then just as quickly looked away, red flooding her cheeks. What had *Mammi* said to her? Paris crossed to the table, but instead of sitting where he indicated, she shook her head. "I know I just took my coat off, but I'm not going to be very *gut* company. I'm sorry. I should go."

What? She couldn't go. He didn't know where she lived, didn't know anything about her, more than her name and birthday. Both important things, but…

"Oh, but your letter." *Mammi* looked around. "You can't leave without it. Your *daed* will think I'm a forgetful old fool."

Daadi chuckled. "It's right here. You put it in the breadbox." He opened it up and handed the envelope to Paris.

"Danki." Paris laid it on the table and put her coat back on. "I'll read it later. I really do need to go. *Danki* again for the dress."

"Oh." *Mammi* turned and hurried into the other room, returning a moment later with the pretty blue dress. She slipped it into a plastic bag. "You can't forget this. Are you sure you can't stay?"

Paris forced a smile. "Positive. But *danki* again." She took the bag and hurried out the door.

Without the letter.

And without another glance in his direction.

"I'll be right back." Quil grabbed his coat off the hook, shoved his arms into the sleeves, picked up the envelope, and went after her. He needed to get his bag out of the buggy anyway. "I'll untether the horse," he called to her as he laid the letter on the front seat, then reached into the backseat of the buggy and removed his bag. "I have something for you. I hate being responsible for your birthday being ruined."

She turned, her expression drawn. "You weren't. Well, not directly."

"Just indirectly?" He unzipped the orange bag and pulled out the plastic sack from the store. He tucked the envelope into the bag with his purchases. "Sure. Open this later. And just so you know, I don't want to enter a relationship on the rebound."

"Of course not. That's commendable. And just so you know, I wasn't expecting a relationship. And I didn't mean to flirt." Her voice was flat.

Had she flirted? If she had, it'd been nothing compared to Sarah. But this wasn't going so well. "I mean, not only you. I don't want a relationship with your friend or anyone."

"You might want to explain that to Sarah. But she's not *gut* at taking *nein* for an answer."

"I—uh." How could he put what he wanted to say into words? He'd just give it a shot. "You intrigue me, Paris Kauffman. I want to see more of you. Can we be friends?"

She hesitated, staring at the ground. Finally, she lifted a shoulder. "Sure. I can never have too many friends. Especially since it seems I've lost one." She frowned, darting a glance his direction. "But you'll have to be careful not to fall in love with me." A fresh influx of color flooded her cheeks. "I didn't mean to say that. I didn't even think it, I just… I don't know. Open mouth and insert foot."

Quil chuckled and held the bag out to her again. "Take it. Sarah pointed out some things you like. And happy birthday from a not-so-secret admirer."

She frowned but took the bag.

"Now I'll go break the news to Sarah that I'm not interested. See you later, Little Miss Birthday Girl."

"You underestimate the power of Sarah's persuasion." Paris turned and climbed into the buggy. "See you at church next Sunday."

"If not before." He untied the horse from the post. "Are you having a birthday party or not?"

"My *daed* has never given me a party. He's always done treasure hunts." She shrugged. "I doubt anything's changed." She took the reins from him and clicked her tongue. The horse tossed her head and backed away.

Quil turned toward the *haus*. He'd ask *Daadi* for Paris's address—and directions—but wait a sufficient amount of time before he contacted her. Just to be sure he was over Priscilla.

Dating and courtship should be taken seriously, not as something to be jumped into on the rebound.

❄

Ten minutes later, Paris pulled the buggy off the road. No one was coming from either direction. Nothing moved, except the tops of trees and snow drifting across the road.

She swiped at her eyes with her gloved hand and reached for

the bag Quil had given her when he'd tucked *Daed*'s note in there with his gifts. She pulled them out. Heart-shaped measuring spoons along with four cookie cutters: a heart, a circle, a star, and a flower. A basic starter set.

It was sweet of Quil to get her something for her birthday. And even though they weren't courting—and never would be—she'd put the cookie cutters and measuring spoons in her hope chest.

He'd also picked up a notebook, the type with hard front and back covers, decorated with tiny conversation hearts. He'd forgotten to take the price tag off, so she scratched at the yellow circle with the price written on it. She loved conversation hearts. Had since kindergarten when Quil had given her a pink package full of candy. Her name was printed on the back of the box, followed by his.

She'd been in love with him since.

It hadn't hurt he'd given her a box every year on Valentine's Day during their school days.

Was this a sign he remembered?

Maybe it was better he didn't. That way she wouldn't need to be embarrassed by how pathetically she'd followed him around, hoping he'd give her a glance. Talk to her. Tease her. Notice her.

He never had.

She moistened her lips with her tongue, then wished she hadn't. It'd cause them to dry out and chap. Or so she'd been told.

She set the notebook next to the cookie cutters on the seat and retrieved the letter. She ran her finger under the edge of the envelope, pulled out the paper, then carefully opened the note.

This one didn't have an address. Instead the instructions: Find Amos Wyse. Where would she find him?

Amos was a handyman who worked wherever he was needed.

She hadn't a clue where to start.

❄

Quil strode back into the *haus* to find Sarah hurrying over, arm outstretched to help him with his coat. He didn't need assistance. Not from her or from anyone.

He stiffened as she took the coat from him, and reached around him, close enough the fabric of her clothes brushed against him and hung the coat on the hook. If only he could say something right now, in a way she'd be able to understand, and end this madness. But it'd be cruel to say anything in front of his grandparents. Besides, he'd already stated, in multiple ways, that he wasn't interested.

Whereas Paris had gotten messages he hadn't intended.

His communication skills must've regressed since graduation. He used to make good grades on his oral and written reports in school.

He sat at the table and prayed Sarah wouldn't sit next to him. To no avail.

She. Was. Too. Close.

Mammi served each of them a slice of pie, filled with thick gooey raisins. Quil almost groaned. No one made raisin pie like *Mammi.* Not even *Mamm,* and she tried and tried. The difference had to be found in the unknown ingredient on the recipe card, because it called for one-third cup _____ and no amount of begging had resulted in finding out the secret.

"Did Paris go on without me?" Sarah poked a finger at the water glass *Daadi* had put on the table. Because her friend was no longer there to jab? A touch of whininess entered her voice.

Quil didn't see why she'd be upset about it because she'd told Paris she'd stay here and give him a tour. Not that he wanted one. Because he didn't. Especially not from Sarah!

Mammi pursed her lips. "Maybe she thought you didn't want to be with her."

"Of course, I did. It's her birthday…"

She kept making noise, but Quil tuned her out. It seemed nothing would make Sarah whatever-her-last-name-was happy.

He went to take a bite, but Sarah touched him on his hand, bumping him hard enough that he fumbled the fork, and the piece of delicious raisin-ness fell to the plate. At least it wasn't wasted.

He glared at Sarah. "What'd you go and do that for?" Though it probably was an accident.

"How will you be able to take me home from her surprise birthday party if we don't know where it is and can't go?" she asked.

Daadi dipped his head, concentrating on the pie. *Mammi* stared at Sarah, a hardness in her eyes that Quil hadn't seen since… well, since Priscilla.

Jah. He wasn't interested in Sarah either.

Mammi had set her hopes on some other girl back in Mio for a granddaughter-in-law.

Quil frowned, trying to remember who it was.

Some other girl, who, for years, came by his grandparents' *haus* in Mio daily to help with the household chores. Some girl who'd assisted with the sales in the winter. He squeezed his eyes shut, trying to "see" her. To remember. A girl who'd moved up here to the Upper Peninsula, leaving *Mammi* sad for days on end and… oh. Oh, no.

The niggling he'd had when he met Paris at the bakery that *morgen* suddenly made sense.

It *was* Paris.

Chapter Five

Paris stared at the paper in her hand. The first and most logical step would be to go by the nearest Amish home and ask if they knew where Amos Wyse was working. Because it was Saturday, he could be at home with his family. The note held no clue.

She glanced around to get a bearing on her location. The mailbox just ahead had tiny stick-on letters: Nehemiah Brunstetter. Bishop Miah usually knew what was happening in the community. She clicked her tongue and guided the horse into the driveway, coming to a stop in front of the barn.

Katherine Brunstetter came out on the porch, wiping her hands on a dishtowel. "Hiya, Paris. What brings you by? Want to come in to warm up for a spell?" She exaggerated a shiver.

Bishop Miah emerged from the barn, adjusting his hat to protect his eyes from the low-lying glare of the winter sun.

"*Danki,* but *nein.* I can't stay. I'm looking for Amos Wyse." Paris fidgeted, hoping they wouldn't get the wrong impression. Perhaps she should explain. "My *daed—*"

"Ask and it shall be given. Seek and ye shall find. Knock and the doors will be opened," the bishop intoned. And with that he turned and went back into the barn.

Bishop Miah had a reputation for quoting random Scripture verses or proverbs that at first appeared to mean nothing, but in hindsight were insightful.

"Hmm. Check his home. He usually helps his *daed* with the chores on Saturday. Or courting some girl… Of course, not at this hour of the day. *Jah,* check there." Katherine flapped the towel at her reddened face. "Are you sure you can't stay for a cup of hot tea and cookies? I've got onions and peppers sautéing and need to stir them before they burn."

"I'm sure. *Danki.*" Paris waved, drove around the circle, and back out to the road.

The Wyse family lived about a mile farther down the road. Paris drove in and parked in front of the *haus.* It seemed quiet, as if no one was home. No one came out of either the barn or the *haus,* but smoke drifted from the chimney.

She got out of the buggy and went into the barn. It seemed the logical first place to look.

A man's voice raised and lowered somewhere in the barn. Because there were frequent pauses and she couldn't hear anyone answer, it was a one-sided conversation, unless he was on the phone. She headed toward the voice.

Amos sat on a stool that could've come straight out of a doctor's office. He twirled around on it, a cell phone held to his ear. He glanced up at Paris's approach and held up a finger in a wordless "wait one."

She nodded and retreated to the entry to give him privacy.

A black-and-orange cat emerged from the shadows and made a figure-eight around Paris's ankles. She crouched down to pet it.

About ten minutes later, Amos walked toward her through the shadows. He slid his cell phone into his pocket as he approached. "You found me." He grinned. "I might have something for you."

Paris laughed. "You might?"

"Nothing tangible. Just verbal." Amos leaned against the wall and crossed his legs at the ankles. "Your *daed* overheard me talking to a couple of the other *youngies* last church Sunday. We were making plans to hire a driver and go to Niagara Falls in New York before we take the classes for church membership. Several other Amish *youngies* from different communities plan to join us. Your *daed* suggested you might like to go." He studied her a moment. "Are you interested? So far there are only three of us from this district, but as soon as word spreads, the van we hired will fill up fast."

"I'd love to. It sounds like so much fun." And it was sweet of *Daed* to think of her. Though his motive was probably to introduce her to more young men from other areas because their community was so small.

"Great." Amos straightened. "I'll add you to the list and be in contact about the final plans."

"Do you have an envelope for me?"

Amos shook his head. "*Nein.* This is the big finale. Happy birthday." He winked. Music came from his pocket, and he pulled his phone out as he walked away.

Should she tell Sarah about this exciting news? Or would it be better to let her find out on her own and think she knew before Paris?

It'd be like rubbing salt into an open wound if Sarah found out from her.

And Quil... her heart lurched. What if he decided to go?

❄

Quil waited until *Daadi* finished his pie and *koffee* and headed back out to the quiet solitude of the barn and *Mammi* went to "finish up a little something" in the back room before he turned to Sarah. Hopefully, this exchange would go better than the one he'd had with Paris less than an hour ago.

He cleared his throat and shifted in the chair. *Gott, help her to hear me.*

She smiled softly, expectancy in her eyes. As if she figured he was ready to propose or ask to court her or something equally serious. When they'd first met? Hardly. Had his cousin Peter started to court her so quickly? *Mammi* had mentioned Peter courting some local flirt—and Sarah's behavior screamed that it'd been her. The rapidness with which he'd moved in on Priscilla seemed to indicate he might have.

Quil shook those thoughts away. "Listen. I'm just coming out of a relationship, and I need time to heal before I begin another with, uh, someone. I'm flattered by your interest, but I'm not ready." He'd never be ready. "Can we keep it as just friends? I don't know anyone here yet, except for you and Paris, and I need friends."

Sarah frowned, but nodded. "We'll be close friends. Best friends. For now. But when you're ready, here I am."

Best friends? If she treated her close friends the way she treated Paris…

And that was another thing. He didn't know how to address her boldness or her unkind attitude toward Paris. Both were major deterrents to any level of friendship. Should he ask *Mammi* to talk to Sarah about it? But he doubted Sarah would listen, and *Mammi* would fret over why he was so concerned about her actions and reactions.

He studied the remnants of pie on his plate, picked up his fork, and stabbed a plump raisin he'd missed. He ate it. *Gott, please, guide my words.*

"I'm not so impressed with what I saw today." He scraped his fork sideways across the plate to get the remnants of the filling.

She bobbed her head in agreement. "*Jah,* that's exactly what I was trying to tell Paris. She may be my best friend, but she's so full of herself. Getting the whole community involved…" She shook her head sadly. "But that reminds me. We'd better take the tour I promised real fast, so we can catch up with Paris and find out where her surprise birthday party is so we can go. And even though we're just friends for now, you can still take me home. That way all the other girls will know you're taken."

His communication skills had definitely gone downhill. Quil sighed. And tried again.

"I'm not so impressed with *your* attitude. You were mean to Paris—on her birthday."

Sarah laughed. "Oh, that. I was just kidding. It's a joke."

"Not funny. And no one was laughing."

Sarah shrugged. "It's not a big deal. It doesn't bother her. Besides, she needed to know she was in the wrong. And I was ever-so-nice about it."

He was pretty sure it had bothered Paris, but she hadn't lost her sweet disposition, not even when telling him to get lost. Not that she'd used those words.

Hold it. Wasn't Sarah contradicting herself?

His brow furrowed. He'd figure it out later. "It bothers me. If you treat your best friend this way, how will you treat your future husband? Especially since you were already rude to me. Think about it awhile. I'm going to help *Daadi.* He's the reason I'm here. You can go on home or find Paris. Let me know if you find out about a birthday party because I'd like to go." Not that he'd take her home.

"I sure will." Sarah's smile was back, even lighting her eyes. "Ever so nice to meet you, Quil." She fluttered her lashes—again—and sashayed out of the room.

His communication skills must've sunk to all-time lows. What had he said to give her the impression she'd gotten instead of the one he'd intended? He'd puzzle it out later.

Quil collected the dirty plates, forks, and mugs and carried them to the sink. The cold water, intended for Paris, he drank.

Sometimes water tasted so *gut.*

As clean and refreshing as the girl it'd been intended for.

His heart rate quickened. Did she still come by here to help *Mammi*?

❄

At home, Paris unhitched the buggy horse, Treasure, and put her in her stall. She wiped her down, then gave her some oats and fresh water. She left the stall and closed the gate.

Daed strode toward her. A big grin appeared as he neared. "You're home. Sooner than I expected."

Paris rushed to him, and he folded her into his hug. "*Danki, Daed*."

"Was it *gut*? Your *mamm* and I had a lot of fun planning this. Your brothers and sisters are even contributing to the, uh…" He hesitated. Frowned. And looked at her as if to gauge whether or not she knew about the trip the *youngies* planned.

"*Jah*. I loved everything. And I'm so excited about the trip to Niagara Falls!"

Daed's grin reappeared. "Your siblings are excited and probably a bit envious, but they all had special trips, camping or traveling, with the *youngie*, so you should get an opportunity, too. What'd Sarah think?"

Paris sobered. "She doesn't know yet. She was a bit upset when she found out Peter wasn't returning because he married, and then his cousin Quil—another one of the Stutzmans' grandsons—got off the bus, and she did what she could to keep the focus on herself. I left her at the Stutzmans'."

"Aquila Stutzman." *Daed* studied her. "So, he's here now."

Was he remembering her childish scribbles on any scrap of paper she could find? Paris and Aquila forever. Paris loves Quil. Hearts with his name written in the center. Maybe he even recalled how she'd begged to volunteer her time to help Quil's sweet *mammi* so she'd be sure to see him on a regular basis.

It hadn't worked then. No reason to expect it would now even if she still did go over once a week to help with laundry and other odd jobs.

Quil didn't remember her.

Paris shrugged. "Sarah's already got her eyes set on him. And he had a girlfriend in Mio. He said something about not wanting to jump into a new relationship."

He might've been telling the truth. Or telling her in a nice way he wasn't interested in her.

But then again, he'd said he was her not-so-secret admirer.

And he'd bought her heart-shaped measuring spoons. Not to mention a journal with conversation hearts decorating the cover. Cookie cutters... She'd bake a dozen cookies for him, complete with icing, to say thanks.

That would upset Sarah. Not if she included Sarah in the gift. He'd said she'd told him what she liked.

Daed walked off, muttering something about broken hearts and shattered dreams.

Paris got her gifts and her unopened Cherry Coke out of the buggy and crossed over the snow-covered driveway to the house. She left her packages on the small table beside the door, took off her outerwear and removed her shoes, then gathered her things.

Mamm came into the kitchen and smiled. "Oh, *gut,* you're home. Phoebe Stutzman told me she chose blue for the dress I asked her to make you." She eyed the bag Paris had stuffed everything into, except the basket. "May I see it?"

Paris opened the bag and pulled it out. She held it up. "I didn't try it on."

Mamm studied it. "It looks as though it should fit. She said it's the perfect shade of blue for a wedding dress, if you want to hold on to it."

Paris's heart lurched at the memory of *Mammi* Phoebe's hug and words about dreams coming true. She forced a laugh. "Except there's no man in the picture."

"There might be, sooner rather than later." A secret smile played on *Mamm*'s mouth. "A little birdie told me—"

The kitchen door opened. Paris lowered the dress she held and turned.

Sarah pulled her coat off. "You accidentally left me behind. I need to know where the party is and what time? We can have one of those hot chocolate sticks and a sliver of fudge while we discuss it."

Mamm made a soft snorting sound.

Paris refolded the dress and returned it to the bag. "There isn't a surprise party. This is it."

Sarah huffed. "Then what is the point of this whole thing? I was looking forward to the party, so Quil could take me home, and everyone would know he's my future husband. He as good as said so, you know."

A quick breath. A forced smile. A please-leave-now-so-I-can-cry-in-private pain stabbed Paris. It was a *gut* thing she hadn't fallen for him again.

Mamm's snort was louder this time. She covered it with a cough, picked up Paris's bag and basket, and turned away. "I'll put these in your room."

Her way of saying the fudge and hot chocolate sticks would not be shared now or later. At least not with Sarah. Which was fine with Paris. Right now, she was tired of being nice and didn't want to lose her temper with her friend.

"I'm happy for you, but you'll have to discreetly show off your new relationship another day and a different way. There's no party." Paris glanced around. Bread dough rose on the counter near the stove. A mixing bowl full of chocolate chip cookie dough waited to be dropped onto cookie sheets.

Sarah huffed again. "Well, I promised Quil I'd let him know the details. But we can't have it at my *haus*. How could he take me home? Maybe we can have it at his grandparents'. I've got to go. Lots of planning to do. Plus, I've got to get the word out. I know,

I'll stop and tell Faith. She's the biggest gossip. She'll let everyone know before I can reach the Stutzmans'. Bye!"

Quil's *Mammi* Phoebe had a big surprise waiting for her.

And Quil wouldn't get any homemade cookies as a thank you.

He and Sarah deserved each other.

A not-so-secret admirer. *Ha.* He was a two-timing louse, just like his cousin.

Chapter Six

Quil found *Daadi* in his makeshift office in the barn, studying papers and making notes.

Daadi glanced up when Quil came in. "Just checking orders. We need to mark trees for harvest, so we can have them delivered to tree lots for the day after Thanksgiving. We have orders coming from most of the major cities." He shuffled some papers. "Nothing from the capitol yet. I hope this will be the year the original farm or this new branch will get an order for the governor's mansion or the capitol building. They order from a different place every year."

The familiar shop talk piqued Quil's interest. He couldn't wait to get started helping with the business—something other than the field labor he did back home. "How can I help?"

Daadi shook his head. "Go clear a path between the barn and the *haus.* We must have a foot of snow. Shovel's in the storage room right on the other side of this room. Have fun." He winked.

Quil chuckled. He retrieved the shovel and had half of the path cleared when a horse and buggy pulled into the drive. He left the shovel in a snow drift and went to investigate. Maybe Paris couldn't bear the thought of being away from him and had come to work for *Mammi*. His heart rate increased.

The door opened, and Sarah emerged.

He cringed. He should've ignored the buggy and continued working.

"We've so much to do. No time for shoveling. There are more important things than that."

"Like what?" He shouldn't have asked. *Daadi* had asked him to shovel so it was important to him and *Mammi*.

Sarah rolled her eyes. "Paris's *daed* didn't plan a birthday party, so I'm throwing her one."

"Oh. That's kind of you."

She smiled. "We have to have it here, though, so you can take me home."

Quil stiffened. "Here? Wait, what? You can't have a birthday party here. This isn't your home, and—"

"Too late. Word is already getting out. Now, I know the *haus* is clean because Paris was out yesterday helping your *mammi* with some chores, but I need to make sure there's a table set up somewhere for the food everyone will bring. We need to plan activities. Is there a hill on this farm where we could sled?"

"If there is, it's covered in Christmas trees. Seriously, Sarah, *nein*. You can't do this. I can't imagine what *Mammi* will say. Besides, she's already planned dinner, and *nein*. Just *nein*."

But Paris still worked for *Mammi*? That was *gut* news. He might see her again the next time she was here. And be able to find out where she lived.

She glared at him. "You're being mean. We *have* to do this. You have to take me home. Besides—"

Quil firmed his jaw and glared at her. "I said *nein*. I will take you to your buggy, but you need to tell everyone the party is off. Or that it will be someplace else. I'm not doing this to my grandparents."

She stomped her foot. Not that it had the effect she probably intended on the snow. "Aquila Stutzman, let's get one thing straight right now. If I'm going to be your *frau,* you need to learn to listen to me. And I said—"

"*Nein.*" Quil bit out. "And furthermore, you are not my future *frau.* Didn't you listen to a word I said earlier?"

"Don't say things you don't mean, Quil. Your *mammi* will see it my way." Sarah smirked, pushed past him, and headed for the *haus.* "*Mammi* Phoebe," she yelled as soon as she opened the door.

Quil retrieved his shovel and resumed clearing the path, with a bit of extra vigor in the scooping and throwing of snow. *Mammi* knew how to say *nein.* She was downright *gut* at it. At least she had been with her grandchildren.

The door slammed shut behind Sarah.

Sarah couldn't talk *Mammi* into doing anything she didn't want to do.

Thirty minutes later, Quil mucked the horse stalls, the stench of the manure reminding him of his bad attitude due to that pushy girl.

Sarah reappeared, a big smile in place. "She said *jah* when I reminded her it'd be a *gut* way to thank Paris for all the hard work she does and for little or no pay."

Quil stiffened. Glared at her. "I don't believe you." There was no way *Mammi* would've given in to someone who was so out-of-control in the emotional-intelligence department.

Sarah smirked. "She suggested we have it in the barn and maybe ice skate on the pond in the pasture. She says it should be frozen solid. I won't skate, because I fell through the ice last winter, and it scared me. I almost drowned, you know. But you and I could take a walk while the others risk their lives."

He'd been in the area, visiting his grandparents last winter when the ice cracked, and the girls had fallen waist deep into the pond. Quil helped pull them out, after he'd tugged two other people to safety. He didn't remember Sarah, though. Probably a *gut* thing. And of course, her claws might've been firmly planted elsewhere, too. Like in Peter, as *Mammi* had suggested in her letter.

Had Paris been at that skating frolic? He shook his head. It didn't matter. His heart and thoughts had been too wrapped up in Priscilla. He hadn't cared much about anyone else back then.

"I'll check the ice when I finish this job." And he'd be in the center of the pond when they were ice skating, so he wouldn't be around Sarah.

"I need to spread the news about needing ice skates and bake cupcakes because it is Paris's birthday. Not that she needs any more attention, but it'll be so worth it when we take our relationship to the next level." Sarah beamed at him.

She still hadn't figured out what *nein* means. Probably thought that because she talked *Mammi* into the party, she could get him to change his mind, too.

Why, why, why did *Mammi* say *jah*? Quil refrained from groaning and turned his back on Sarah. "I'll let you get to it then."

He'd finish his job, then go quiz *Mammi* to get answers. And directions to Paris's home so he could pick her up for the surprise party.

Sarah would probably forget to invite her on purpose.

❄

That afternoon, Paris went to the basement to fold laundry. Some Amish hung laundry outside year round, but their old farmhouse boasted the blessing of a woodstove in the basement—used only in the winter—and there wasn't any point in wasting that heat. Of course, it also helped keep the upstairs warmer too. It was an opportunity to sulk without witnesses, too, with Sarah laying instant claim to Quil.

She'd almost finished folding the dresses when *Mamm* appeared in the open doorway above the stairs.

"Paris? Someone is here to see you." Her voice was strained.

Unusual. She usually didn't announce her friends—just sent them to find her. And never had one stressed her out before.

"I'll be right up. I'm almost finished."

"I'll send him down." There was a definite note of tension in her voice.

Odd. And… him?

Paris paused mid-fold and looked up as another, larger shadow filled the doorway above.

The steps creaked as he—whoever he was—made his way down.

Mamm left the door open. Paris finished folding the dress and moved the lantern closer. It cast shadows across…Quil's face.

Paris's heart pounded. Her palms grew sweaty. At least it explained the tension in *Mamm*'s voice. She was afraid of Paris's crush resurrecting and her having another broken heart. She steeled herself and found a smile. "Hey. I wasn't expecting to see you."

"I know. *Mammi* told me how to get here. She said to tell you you're needed for a while this evening. I already told your *mamm* and *daed*." He moistened his lips.

"Needed? For what? I was there yesterday *morgen*. She could've asked me to do it then."

Quil hesitated a moment before he shrugged. "She didn't know…um, expect that…um, well, to need you."

Something was off. Quil never stuttered. Was she making him nervous? He'd always been the one to make her stutter and stumble.

Paris turned her attention back to the clothesline and scanned it to make sure there weren't any unmentionables hanging in plain sight. Nothing too shocking dangled from the line. Just a few more dresses and a short row of *Daed*'s work shirts.

She unpinned the next item. "What does she need me for?"

"Uh, she didn't exactly say. Just that you should expect to stay for supper."

Even stranger. Paris frowned. Hopefully, *Mammi* Phoebe wasn't trying any matchmaker schemes tonight. "Okay. I'll be there as soon as I finish." She unpinned the next dress. "I won't be long."

Quil shifted uncomfortably. "She sent me to pick you up." He moved to the end of the line and unpinned one of *Daed*'s shirts. Then he stared down at it, frowning, as if he wasn't sure how to go about folding it. Or maybe as if he'd overstepped an invisible boundary.

He had. A couple of them, actually.

"I don't need a ride." Especially if he was an unwilling chauffeur. Paris put the dress in the basket and reached for the last one.

"*Mammi* said not to return without you. I'll bring you back home afterwards, of course." He awkwardly folded the shirt and put it in the basket.

How many times had she foolishly dreamed of him giving her a ride in his buggy? Was she dreaming, or was this an unexpected birthday surprise that even *Daed* couldn't have planned? Sarah would have major issues with it when she found out. Though, Quil probably only offered her a ride because his *mammi* insisted, and not because he truly wanted to. And Paris didn't want to spend time with him because of his *mammi*'s pity. Or to make Sarah jealous.

Paris resisted the urge to check to make sure Quil had folded *Daed*'s shirt right. *Daed* wouldn't complain, and she appreciated the help. She reached for a shirt at the same time he unpinned the one beside it, and their fingers brushed. Electricity zinged through her. She jerked away, leaving the shirt dangling from one pin, as the other wooden peg tumbled to the floor.

Quil made some sort of sound she couldn't identify before it morphed into a chuckle. Had he felt it, too, or was he laughing at her for being so clumsy? Just like Sarah did more often than not?

Paris couldn't look at him. She bent to pick up the clothespin and unpinned the other, then deftly folded the shirt.

He added the last shirt to the basket and picked it up. "I'll carry this upstairs for you."

She nodded, hoping he didn't notice her burning cheeks. She pressed her hands to her face as he started upstairs. *Lord, give me strength. Help me not to fall in love with him. Again.*

She extinguished one lantern and carried the other upstairs. Quil had left the basket on a dining room chair.

With a metal spatula, *Mamm* lifted a couple cookies from the metal cooling racks. She held them out to Quil.

He took them off the spatula and bit into of one of them. "*Danki. Sur gut.*"

Mamm beamed. "You're welcome. So glad you were able to come and help your grandparents. I'm sure you'll love it here."

"I hope so. My grandparents intend for one of their grandsons to take over this tree farm. No reason it shouldn't be me. The one in Mio supports my *daed,* three *onkels,* and a few of my older cousins, and the income can't be divided any more without hurting everyone." He shrugged, his gaze resting on Paris for a brief second, before returning to *Mamm.* "It'll do me *gut* to get away from there, and my grandparents definitely need me."

"*Jah.*" *Mamm* frowned. "I heard, of course, about your girlfriend marrying your cousin. I'm sorry. It must've hurt."

Paris hated that he'd gotten hurt by someone. As badly as she'd ached over Quil never noticing her, she wouldn't wish it on anyone.

Quil dipped his head. "It's for the best. It hurt, but... She didn't truly love me. And I...well, now I wonder if I truly loved her or if it was only...something else. It doesn't matter. What matters are my grandparents. Family. And, unless *Gott* leads differently, I need to be here to help."

Paris nodded. They did need help. And she was glad to do her part. Always had been, though she'd initially wanted to work for them to get Quil's attention rather than for some nobler reason. She'd grown up since then.

Quil's attention was worthless. Especially since he turned it so quickly to Sarah.

Not that she begrudged Sarah for winning him so quickly.

Or maybe she did.

Vanity. All vanity.

Mamm smiled brightly. "Well, you two go and have fun. I'll leave a lantern burning on the kitchen table, Paris."

"I shouldn't be that late. It's just an odd job *Mammi* Phoebe needs me to do. I won't stay for supper. In fact, Quil, I really insist on driving myself there. That way I can come straight home and not bother you for a ride."

"No bother. I don't mind at all," he said.

Mamm's hands fluttered. "I'd feel ever so much better if you rode with Quil. Especially with it getting dark so early. I don't want to worry about a vehicle hitting you or the buggy and being all alone."

Really? Since when? What had Quil said to *Mamm* for her to give in so easily?

Quil winked. "That settles it. I'll keep you safe, Paris."

She lifted her coat and bonnet off the hook.

He'd keep her safe, maybe. That wasn't a concern. While a trip to the Stutzmans' wasn't exactly a party, she needed to be careful not to get too close to Quil on her birthday or else her heart would start to believe he was her gift.

❄

By the time Quil drove back into the driveway at the tree farm, *youngies* had already gathered. The outline of black buggies and sleighs filled the neighbor's snow-covered cornfield. If Paris noticed the buggies, she never said a word. Nor did she move from her huddled position against the far side of the carriage. Was she afraid of accidentally bumping into him? Resisting the urge to take the final curve fast, he kept it slow and steady until he parked in front of the shed. He set the brakes, climbed out, and turned to assist Paris. But she clambered out and set her eyes on the *haus.*

"I'll just go see what *Mammi* Phoebe needs." She pushed past him.

Quil caught her shoulder. The same electricity as before zinged through him. How had he never noticed her before? Especially because he'd never felt this same way around Priscilla? "I… uh, believe what she needed is in the barn."

Paris squinted as she turned toward him. "Quil, what's going on?"

He looked away, afraid she'd see the secrets in his eyes. "Let's go see." He reached for the sliding door and gave it a hard push, revealing the pitch-black darkness of the interior.

"I don't think she's in there." Paris backed away with a glance up toward the rafters as if she expected a bat to swoop down. It happened occasionally.

He swung an arm out to stop her. It landed—unintentionally—around her shoulders. He let it stay—intentionally. Because it felt right. And he wanted to hold her.

She jerked to a stop and stared up at him. Trembling.

His brain cells packed up and left for vacation.

"Happy birthday!" The cry rose at the same time lanterns and flashlights flickered to life.

Paris stumbled forward a step and burst into tears. She turned away, her face buried in her hands.

Quil took half a step forward, wrapped his arms around her, and pulled her against his chest. For a millisecond, she clung to him, crying, but then his hand accidentally slid from her upper back to about midway down. His heart pounded into overdrive. If only they were alone.

His touch must've shocked her to her senses. She stiffened and pushed against his chest.

He let her go, even though he wanted to hold her tight and

never let go. What other choice did he have with the others surging forward?

The other girls there—he didn't know any of them—gathered around Paris, talking and giggling as they linked arms and drew her into the barn.

Leaving him no choice but to follow and pray Sarah wouldn't find him.

But… he glanced toward the table he'd set up for goodies per *Mammi*'s request. No cupcakes were there. And even though he didn't know Sarah well, he figured she'd be first in line to welcome Paris and take credit for the party. She must be running late.

That was a blessing.

Someone had brought a picnic jug full of hot water as well as packets of hot chocolate, tea bags, apple cider, and instant *koffee,* setting them up at the end of the table next to a stack of insulated disposable cups. An appetizing display of sandwiches cut into fourths, raw vegetables, cookies, brownies, and other finger-foods filled the rest of the table.

A tall man with reddish hair appeared at Quil's side. "You're new here. I'm Amos Wyse. And that"—he indicated another man with brown hair hovering near a woman— "that's my friend Noah Behr with Arie Zimmerman. Come on. I'll introduce you to everyone."

"Aquila Stutzman. My friends call me Quil." He glanced around for Paris and found her in the center of a gaggle of girls, all of them laughing and talking. Sarah wasn't with them. But he recognized Agnes from the candy store. Arie headed that way, maneuvering her way through the crowd to Paris's side where she wrapped her in a hug.

Paris was well-liked.

It was probably a *gut* thing Sarah had planned a spur of the moment surprise party, even though her intentions weren't the best. When he saw her, he'd tell her so.

But Amos was still talking, leading Quil through a maze of *youngies,* rattling off names as he went. Quil wouldn't remember most of them two minutes from now.

"Some of us brought sleighs. I'm sure you saw them. I was thinking it'd be fun to take sleigh rides down to the pond to go skating. Were you able to get Paris's skates?"

"*Jah,* I asked her *daed* for them when I went to pick her up."

Amos stilled a second. "Did Paris mention the trip to Niagara Falls? We're trying to get it organized. Are you interested? Paris is going."

Was Amos courting Paris? A sick pit formed in Quil's stomach. He couldn't lose her now. Not when he just found her again. Not when his arms could still feel her cradled against his chest.

"Ah, *nein,* she didn't mention it. It sounds fun, and I'd love to be included, but I'd have to clear it with my grandparents." They'd probably say *no*. It was going into the busy season.

Amos smiled. "Awesome. Hope you can come. We have Noah, Arie, Paris, me, and Mose Graber going so far. One of the drivers owns a big van that seats twelve, including the driver. We're trying to fill it up. I think Sarah will want to go. She does everything Paris does." He looked around. "It's strange she isn't here yet. I'll take my buggy over to her *haus* to see if she lost her shoes. She does that routinely." He chuckled. "See you later."

Left alone, Quil glanced around. He wanted to join the girls, edge up next to Paris, and soak in her nearness. But no men were in the circle surrounding her. Noah caught his eye. He looked lost without Arie by his side.

Quil headed in his direction. "Noah, right? I'm a bit overwhelmed. All these people. But I'll get to know everyone eventually." He hoped.

Noah turned to him. "*Jah,* you will. I've been here a year, but spent some time fighting fires in California this year. So, I'm still getting to know folks myself. I'm going to get something to eat and drink. You're welcome to tag along."

"*Danki*." With one last glance toward the talking girls, Quil followed Noah to the food and drink table. He selected a roast beef and mustard sandwich, a handful of sour cream-and-onion potato chips, and a few baby carrots. Then he took a couple of chocolate chip cookies that looked like the ones Paris's *mamm* had given him. He poured hot water into a cup, then grabbed a packet of apple cider mix with cinnamon.

No doubt the real stuff would be better, but this would do.

He found a seat next to Noah on a square bale of hay, set his drink beside him, and balanced his plate on his lap. He'd just finished his sandwich when Amos burst back into the barn, eyes wide.

"Is Sarah here yet?" He scanned the room. "We need to form a search party. Her *mamm* said she left with a platter full of cupcakes over an hour ago."

Chapter Seven

Worried, Paris hurried after Amos to his sleigh. He assisted her into the front seat. Quil climbed into the backseat without waiting for an invitation. She was glad he came along, although he was probably only there because of his feelings for Sarah. It'd been really nice of Sarah to throw a surprise party for her, especially after all the earlier comments, even though she'd only done it to show off her relationship with Quil.

Sarah's conspicuous absence made sense now though. But what was with Quil's lack of concern for his new girlfriend? Though maybe he was trying to pretend so their relationship would be less obvious. And why was Amos so upset? Though, it wasn't like Sarah to miss a party. Especially with Quil there to grab.

Noah approached with Arie by his side. "I'll see if Sarah went to the pond instead. Maybe she thought we were meeting there first."

"She might've. Word went around that we were going ice-skating." Amos nodded. "I checked the foot trail between the Stutzmans' and Sarah's *haus* earlier because everyone knows the shortest distance between two points is a straight line."

True, but Paris had never known Sarah to care about any proven mathematical fact. She'd always been more interested in boys. Especially the one sitting right behind Paris. Besides, Sarah was terrified of the woods after dusk, saying something about "effalonts and woozels," whatever they were. Unless, of course, Peter had been with her. Paris still burned with embarrassment when she recalled Sarah's whispered confessions about her moments alone with Peter. Of course, Sarah might've been lying, too. Surely, they wouldn't have done what Sarah whispered about.

"I thought we'd go by the main road this time." Amos frowned, his brows drawing together.

Midway to Sarah's *haus*, something yellow flashed in the buggy lights. Paris squinted. Was that Sarah's covered yellow plastic platter tipped sideways in a drift?

"Stop! That's Sarah's cupcake carrier." Paris stood in the sleigh, teetering as Amos jerked the reins.

"Whoa!"

Paris jumped out and ran toward the carrier, looking around for Sarah or for footprints. "It doesn't make sense for her to leave this here. Oh, I hope she's okay." She hated the wail that escaped with her words. Had Sarah been kidnapped? That'd happened in other Amish communities.

Amos held a lantern flashlight high, illuminating the ground. His expression was grim, a muscle jumping in his jaw.

Quil followed them. "Look. There's a single set of footprints headed off into the woods. She's following something. Let me see the light."

Amos came closer and held it lower to the ground. "It looks like a small dog or a puppy. Or a pack of them. At least the prints aren't very large."

Quil frowned. "Should we—"

Amos took off running through the woods. "Sarah!"

"Stay here," Quil ordered Paris. He picked up an old quilt and handed it to her. "Get into the sleigh, cover up with a blanket, and don't leave." He darted after Amos, silently. Of course, Amos made enough noise for both of them.

Paris looked down at her tennis shoes. Woefully inadequate in the snow. She'd end up with frostbite. Staying in the sleigh was the wise thing. But obeying Quil rankled her. Who was he to boss her around?

It'd be worth the eventual scolding to make sure Sarah was safe. She tossed the quilt back into the sleigh, hitched up her skirt, and followed the two men. She should've thought to grab her gloves and black bonnet she'd taken off inside the barn. But at least she still wore her coat. The barn wasn't warm enough to shuck her coat at this hour of the night. Not in November. But she'd been so overcome with happiness she hadn't given the temperature another thought.

"Sarah!"

The men were out of sight. Paris quickened her pace, stumbling through the darkness, trying to follow the sound of Amos' voice and the snow crunching beneath their running feet.

She couldn't hear any answering calls, though.

Lord, let her be okay.

Why would Sarah abandon her cupcakes and chase a bunch of puppies? Had she wanted to catch one as a gift? And why hadn't she returned?

Snow seeped into the tops of Paris's shoes, soaking her socks.

"Sarah!" The shout came from a distance.

She needed to catch up with them. Paris increased her speed, tripped over something in the snow, and slammed forward. She threw out her arms to break the fall. Her hands slapped a thin layer of ice, before breaking through into running spring water. Her palms rammed into the rocks at the bottom.

Moisture seeped through her coat, through her dress, saturating her chest to her waist. She pushed herself upright. Her knees and palms burned from contact.

"Quil! Amos!" Her voice wasn't as loud as she'd have liked.

There was no way either man could hear her.

"Sarah!" Amos' yell was faint.

She'd go back to the sleigh, wrap up in the quilt, and wait there. Pretend she'd never left. Paris would spend her time in prayer until they found Sarah.

She took a step, and her knee buckled. Fresh waves of pain worked through her.

But she wouldn't let this stop her.

She had to save herself.

❄

Quil followed Amos until he stumbled to a stop beside a gurgling creek. A thin layer of ice coated it. Quil bent double, trying to catch his breath.

Amos wasn't concentrating on breathing. Instead, he dropped the lantern into the snow and waded into the creek. "Sarah."

What? Quil picked up the flashlight and held it high. Sarah lay, half in the water, half out, a Border collie puppy held tightly in her arms.

Her teeth chattered so hard she didn't try to speak. The puppy struggled weakly to get away.

Amos grabbed the pup, turned, and thrust it at Quil.

He took the baby animal that seemed unhappy about its change of location. Even if it was better than a cold bed of not-quite-frozen water. The pond might've been frozen deeply enough to safely skate on, but running water, not so much. The puppy weakly whined, alternately kicking, then staying stiff as a board.

Amos bent, scooped Sarah up in his arms, and turned. "Can you carry the dog and the light?"

Quil was glad Amos was carrying her, but what about Paris? Or was Amos the heroic type who liked to rescue everyone?

"Don't let him go," Sarah chattered. "They dumped a litter of puppies on the road. Four of them. We need to find the rest. I think I saw them over—"

"Shh. Don't talk." Amos pulled her closer. "We'll get you to safety first, and then go look for the rest of the pups."

Sarah wrapped an arm around Amos' neck and held on.

"Go on ahead." Amos made a motion with his head. "Light the way for us."

Quil nodded but wasn't sure how effective he'd be with a fighting, crying puppy and a lantern.

He followed the trail of boot prints out to the sleigh and froze when the vehicle loomed empty before him. He caught his breath. There was no sign of Paris.

Amos lifted Sarah into the sled, tucked a blanket around her, then grabbed the plastic dish she had left earlier. "Where's Paris?" Concern filled his voice.

"I don't know. I told her to stay here. I'm going to look for her." Quil scanned the ground closer to the woods. It'd be hard to find her trail, but she must've lost theirs at some point, or they would've found her on the return trip. "Go ahead and make sure Sarah is safe. I'll look for Paris."

Amos could be Sarah's hero. Quil would do his best to become Paris's.

"I'll take Sarah home." Amos took the puppy from Quil. "I'll be back for you and Paris."

"And the puppies. I want to raise the puppies," Sarah said, her teeth chattering.

Amos shook his head. "I'm pretty sure he'll need round the clock feedings. He's pretty young. I'm bottle feeding a rejected calf now. Won't make any difference to add another."

Sarah tugged the blanket higher as Amos put the puppy on her lap. He whined noisily.

"You poor thing. I won't let those bad men take you." Somehow, she untangled her arms while remaining covered and clasped the dog tightly. "Quil, you must find those other three puppies. They'll freeze to death."

And Paris wouldn't?

"I'll be back." Amos jogged around the horse.

Quil shivered in a brisk gust of wind but held the lantern flashlight closer to the ground and took the first step into the woods.

Lord, guide my steps.

❄

Paris struggled to her feet again, grabbed a fallen tree limb to use as a walking stick, and started the return trip. Or what she hoped was the return trip. Slowly. Very slowly. If only she had a flashlight. But she didn't. In the darkness everything looked the same.

She should've listened to Quil. He'd only been looking out for her.

She stopped frequently to listen for Amos' shout, or Quil's voice, but heard nothing.

"Amos! Quil!" She tried shouting again.

Silence.

She wasn't sure how much time passed before a faint call came. "Paris!"

Tears burned her eyes. She sank to the ground. Her leg needed a rest anyway, and she was cold, so cold.

"Help!"

Silence.

She wrapped her arms around herself, tucking her bare hands inside her stiff coat sleeves.

"Paris?" The shout was closer. It sounded like Quil, but it couldn't be. Surely, she must be hallucinating from the cold. Sarah would never allow him to leave her side after this disaster.

Paris was okay with Amos finding her. More than okay. Amos

would be better in so many ways. Because then she wouldn't be in Quil's debt.

But she wanted Quil to be her hero.

Tears seeped, unbidden, from the corners of her eyes and froze on her cheeks.

A bobbing light shone through the darkness. It swung in a wide arc, blinding her.

Quil would never come looking for her when he had Sarah, but someone had. Someone would keep her from freezing to death on her birthday. Someone was her hero, even if it was Amos.

"I'm here." She choked out. "I'm so happy you found me, I could kiss you."

Chapter Eight

His heart stuttering, Quil stumbled to a stop, the flashlight still aimed on Paris. *Jah,* he might just let her kiss him…

Unbidden, his gaze skittered to her lips. He forced it up and gazed into her eyes. With her belief he was looking only for a fling —like his cousin, Peter—it'd be better to pass up this golden opportunity.

If, or when, he kissed her—or anyone—he needed it to mean something.

"I'm honored." His voice emerged raspy. He cleared his throat. "But I won't hold you to it. Yet. Maybe someday. As much as I am intrigued by you, Little Miss Birthday Girl, we aren't exactly at the kissing stage in our relationship."

Ugh. Did he sound as formal and stiff to her as he did to himself? Maybe it would've been better to dash right over there, drop down next to her, and see where it led.

He quivered but forced himself to stand still. He'd done the right thing.

"Quil." Her voice sounded strangled. The lantern highlighted the red flooding her cheeks. "I thought you were someone else."

Amos? Quil opened his mouth. Shut it. So that's the way it was. It surprised him how much it hurt.

"You're blinding me." She put her bare hands over her face.

"Sorry." He dimmed the light, set it on the ground, and approached her. "Amos went with Sarah. He's going to come back for us. Why didn't you stay in the sleigh like I asked?"

She barked a laugh. "You didn't *ask*. You told. And I wanted to be sure Sarah was okay."

He stopped in front of her, pulled his gloves off, and stuffed them into his pocket. "She'll be fine. I think. She rescued a puppy. I'm worried about you. You haven't even tried to stand. Are you okay?" Would he have a reason to carry her in his arms like Amos had carried Sarah?

"A puppy?" Paris stared up at him, still not moving.

"She said someone dumped a litter. Maybe four puppies. Only found one though."

Paris glanced around. "The puppies will freeze to death if they aren't rescued."

Oh. Oh, no. Quil sighed. "Do you know how hard it'll be to find a litter of puppies in the woods after dark?"

"We have to try." She put her palms flat on the ground and pushed herself up. She stumbled, and he reached out to steady her, his hands landing in the vicinity of her armpits. She twisted a little and grabbed the walking stick. "Lead the way."

"Sure." Except he didn't know where to start. Well, other than releasing her, but he didn't want to do that. Instead, he wanted to tug her into his arms and let her give him the kiss she'd offered.

Well, she thought he was someone else, so she didn't really offer it to him.

The kiss he rejected.

Was it too late for a do-over?

"A moment gone is lost forever," he whispered.

"What?" She stepped out of his loose grasp.

His hands slid across her coat. He looked down. His hands were… "You're wet. Icy."

Paris shrugged. "Only a little. I'll be fine."

"It's beyond freezing out here. We've got to get you someplace to warm up. You could get hypothermia." Someone had to take care of her. It might as well be him. But the chances of her listening? Not *gut*. Especially because she was as interested in the puppies as Sarah had been. Quil sighed. "Where do you suggest looking for those puppies?"

"Where did you find Sarah?" She arched a brow. "That'd be where I'd start."

He nodded, took a step, then stopped. "I've a better idea. Let's pray. *Gott* knows where they are. He can help us find them."

"He can lead us directly to them." Paris smiled brightly. She must've curled her hands up, because they disappeared into her sleeves.

He should've offered her his gloves. Except she'd reject them.

He shoved his hand into his pocket and closed it around the gloves. He squeezed them, trying to think of how to word his request, so she'd think she had the option of refusing.

Which, of course, she did.

He sighed, pulled out the gloves, and slid one on his hand. He held the other one out. "Please put this on."

Her eyes narrowed. "You aren't going to offer me both?"

He'd never figure out women.

"Well," he said. "You can put it on, and we can hold hands as we walk. That way all four of our hands will be warm." The idea came out of nowhere. But he liked it. A lot.

She hesitated. Handed him the walking stick. Then, slowly took the offered glove from his fingers and slid it on. He closed his hand around her icy one. His heart fluttered. His stomach clenched. He slid their clasped hands into his coat pocket.

It should be okay. He hoped.

"Now, let's find those dogs."

❄

She was the queen of stupid ideas. There wasn't any way they'd find three puppies in the dark woods at night. Except as they settled into a comfortable stride—even though she limped a little —his flashlight lighting the way, her hand finally warm and snug against his in his pocket, she couldn't think of anyplace else she'd rather be.

Except maybe in his arms.

And he'd rejected that. Rejected her kiss. Rejected her.

At least he was somewhat polite about it. And she'd tried to cover her embarrassment by making some wild claim about thinking he was someone else, when he was the only man she'd ever thought of that way.

She wasn't sure how long they wandered, hand-in-hand through the woods before they came to the spring that was valiantly struggling not to freeze. The one she'd tumbled into when she tried to catch up with Quil and Amos. Except at a different place.

"I think this is where we found Sarah and the puppy. And she said something about the others going…" He looked around. "Amos told her not to talk. And she actually listened." Something that might've been awe filled Quil's voice. "I wonder how he managed it."

Paris giggled.

He clasped her hand tighter, his fingers straightening, shifting, then entwining with hers.

Sarah must never find out. This would fuel Paris's dreams for days. Weeks. Months. Maybe even years. Walking hand-in-hand with Quil in the silent woods on a snowy night.

Except… what was that sound? She stopped.

"I think I heard a whimper," Quil whispered. He released her hand—odd that she immediately missed his touch—and held the lantern high. Then he abruptly dropped to his knees in the snow, put the lantern down, and made kissy sounds.

Nothing happened for a long moment.

Quil made more kissy noises, then suddenly, three tiny black-and-white puppies tumbled out of a hollow log. Their eyes were opened, but they had the roly-poly look of very young puppies.

"Oh, aren't they cute." Paris squealed. She crouched beside Quil and drew the puppies into her arms. "They're wet. We need to get them back to your home and warmed up fast. They'll freeze to death out here." She shivered as the wind whipped her wet clothes along her torso.

Funny how she hadn't noticed it with the warmth of his hand around hers, their walk and her imagination heating her up.

Another movement caught her eye and a fourth black-and-white—

Quil dropped, flung out his arm, knocking her flat on the snow.

"Oof. Hey! What do you think you—?"

"Shhh." He rolled over next to her, pulling her and her bundle of puppies next to him. His hand clasped her neck and applied enough pressure to hide her face against him. "Don't move," he hissed.

She gasped. The puppies clambered over her, and all she could focus on was Quil's nearness. The fresh, outdoorsy pine scent of him.

She trembled.

"Quil! Paris!" a shout came from somewhere close.

She opened her mouth and drew in enough air to shout a response, but a foul smell wafted in the breeze.

Paris willingly moved closer to Quil. "Ugh. You don't smell like fried chicken anymore."

He made a sound that might've been a chuckle. "You sure don't smell like vanilla."

And then his lips touched hers.

It might've been an accident, because he stilled. Jerked back. Sucked in a breath. And then his hand slid from the back of her neck to her cheek, lingered, gently stroking. His wide blue eyes—illuminated by the lantern—met hers.

Hers drifted shut. If this was a dream—which it might be, except for the stench—she didn't want it to end.

A breath whispered between them, and Quil's lips brushed hers. His fingers trembled against her skin.

❄

"Paris! Quil!" The voice was closer. "Ugh, skunk."

Quil rolled away from Paris and sat up. He scrambled to his feet as Amos came into view. "I found her. And the puppies." His stomach ached and not just from the odor. He'd kissed Amos' girl. He'd also fed Paris's belief he was looking for a fling.

Amos snorted. "You found far more than the girl and the puppies. What'd you do, roll in a snowdrift with a skunk?"

"I think the skunk missed us." Not that Quil would complain about its bad aim.

Paris somehow had managed to stand, still clutching three squirmy puppies. "As a matter of fact, we did roll in the snow. Except the skunk wasn't invited. Where's Sarah?"

"At Quil's *mammi*'s *haus.* I offered to take her home, but she insisted she had to go there," Amos said. "And Phoebe said there's a pail full of warm water waiting for you, too, Paris." He reached for the puppies. "I'll take them home with me after I drop you and Quil off. We're bottle-feeding a calf. Four little puppies won't make any difference. We want to keep them safe."

"Go ahead and take me home, too, Amos. I…my parents will be worried." Paris held out the last puppy.

"Your parents know exactly where you are, Little Miss Birthday Girl," Quil said quietly. "I'll take you home, if you don't mind."

And there he'd flung the gauntlet into their court. If Amos courted her, he'd know in about three…two…one…

"I'll take Sarah home then," Amos said, a happy lilt in his voice. "She'll be glad to know the pups are all found and will want to see them settled even if they're at my place and not hers. Yet."

He didn't seem dismayed at all. And… Quil glanced at Paris. She looked almost pleased.

Amos and Paris weren't a couple. Relief filled Quil.

Against his will, his gaze slid farther south to her lips. That brief taste of her sweetness wasn't enough. He wanted more.

Chapter Nine

Quil wanted to scoop Paris up in his arms and carry her out of the woods the way Amos had Sarah, but he didn't have the same excuse. Even though Paris appeared to favor one leg, she seemed to get along okay.

With a sigh, he handed her both of his gloves, took one of the puppies from Amos and, carrying the lantern, led the way back to the sleigh. The odor from the skunk faded the farther they moved away from it. He placed the puppy in the backseat and reached to assist Paris. Her teeth chattered. Poor thing. Maybe it'd warmed her more when he'd held one of her hands in his pocket.

That'd certainly warmed him.

When she was settled next to the three puppies, he covered her with the quilt and climbed in next to her, tucking the quilt over himself as well. He settled as close to her as he could, his leg pressing against hers, and wrapped his arm around her shoulder. Because body heat, right? He had to try to warm her up. And stake a public claim with Amos.

The other man glanced back at them with a grin, then drove on.

And she didn't object. The puppies scampered over them both, wobbling and tumbling, like nothing had happened. They were so cute. And actually worth the tumble in the snow, the skunk, and the kiss.

Amos stopped the sleigh in front of Quil's grandparents' *haus*, and Quil helped Paris out. Whatever else came of this, being lost in the woods had enabled him to assist her. At least for now.

Mammi came out on the front porch, clutching a bath towel. "Oh, you poor thing. Getting lost in the woods and on your birthday, even. Come in. I'll take care of you." She wrapped her arm around Paris's waist and led her into the *haus.*

Quil would've liked the opportunity to do more. He looked at the quiet barn. The birthday party was likely over, so he went to send anyone who was still here home. No one was there. He checked on the animals. Everything had already been done—maybe by *Daadi*—so he headed back inside.

Mammi already had Paris's shoes, socks, and coat off, and had her feet in a bucket of warm water. Amos held Sarah's coat for her, helping her get ready to go. She was all beams and smiles, but at least this time they were directed at Amos.

"I'm going to get the first aid kit. The poor dear scraped her knee." *Mammi* hurried toward another room.

"I told her I was fine." Paris's gaze shot to him.

Quil's lips quirked. "Let her baby you." He opened the door for Sarah and Amos. "Glad you were able to have a surprise party for Paris. It was really nice of you. Even if it didn't turn out exactly as planned."

Sarah's smile rested on him. "*Jah.* It turned out even better." Her lashes fluttered.

Quil's heart stalled. *Not again.*

"Amos told me about the upcoming trip to Niagara Falls. I told him I'd love to go. All four puppies were found. And..." Her smile wattage increased. "Things are looking positive."

He wouldn't ask how. Instead he forced a smile. "*Gut.*" And shut the door behind them.

He pulled a chair over to the bucket at Paris's feet and glanced over his shoulder to make sure *Mammi* hadn't returned yet. "We need to talk," he said quietly.

Paris stiffened and wouldn't meet his gaze. "I understand it was an accident and won't happen again. I shouldn't have said what I did about kissing you anyway. I might've hugged you though." Her lips quirked, the smile appearing and disappearing.

He had intended to say the part about it initially being an accident, but not how it wouldn't happen again, and he didn't want to hear that. Not from her. Because truthfully, he wanted more than the brief taste he'd had in the woods. "I'll take the hug. I'll take another kiss, too. That was…nice." His gaze lowered to her lips.

"Nice." The single word came out flat, but color crept into her cheeks.

"It might've been amazing. I can do better." His own cheeks warmed. "But we were interrupted."

"I won't be your fling," she whispered. There was a strangled note in her voice, as if, maybe...

Jah! She wanted to be more to him than a fling. He warmed from the inside out.

Quil opened his mouth to answer, though he wasn't quite sure how. *Mammi* bustled back into the room with the first aid kit, saving him from a complete insertion of his foot into his mouth.

He didn't want Paris to be his fling. He wanted her to be his… girlfriend. Fiancée. *Frau.* Someday. But it was much too soon to think of courting or marriage on the day he met her—make that noticed her—for the first time. He definitely wanted to know everything about her.

But how on earth did he bring up their shared past and ask her about her history, family, life, when he should know the answers already? *Should* being the keyword. He didn't, due to Priscilla's knack of getting his attention focused solely on her and her physical beauty. The Bible spoke of that very thing in Proverbs. "Favour is deceitful, and beauty is vain: but a woman that feareth the Lord, she shall be praised." Could it be King Solomon had a Priscilla in his life, too, and knew firsthand?

Quil's stomach knotted again.

Mammi's hand lowered to his shoulder and squeezed, getting his attention. "If you move, *Gross-sohn*, I'll bandage Paris's knee. Unless, of course, you want to do it?" There was a hearty dose of humor in her words, as if she'd asked him to move multiple times and he'd been so lost in his thoughts he hadn't heard her.

Thing was, he did want to do it. He wanted to take care of her now and forever.

Paris's hand slid over her dress and cupped her knee protectively; as if afraid he'd lift her dress and start doctoring her. But *Mammi* clearly meant for him to get out of her way, so he got up, checked the kettle on the woodstove, and found homemade hot cocoa. He gave it a swirl with the wooden spoon. Skin had begun to form on top. "Is this ready?"

"I forgot all about it." *Mammi* half-stood from the chair he'd recently vacated.

"I've got it." Quill got out a ladle and filled a mug for Paris. "Do you want some, *Mammi*?"

"*Jah*, and *Daadi* would like some, too." *Mammi* jerked a thumb over her shoulder. "He's in the other room reading *The Budget*."

"Got it." Quil filled another mug for *Mammi* and approached just as she lifted the hem of Paris's dress enough to gently wash the injured knee with a soapy washcloth.

Paris's cheeks flamed brighter, and she twisted her hands in the towel she held.

The scrape was ugly, and bruising had already started. Sarah probably would've milked it, insisting on attention. Paris had powered on. He admired her.

Quil handed her the mug. "Careful. It's hot."

She nodded. "*Danki*."

He put *Mammi*'s mug on the table and went back to retrieve

Daadi's. Quil would preserve Paris's modesty and join *Daadi* in the living room. "Let me know when you're ready to go."

"She can go as soon as we get her bandaged. She's stopped shivering already. But I'd suggest not taking the scenic route home. This time." *Mammi* reached for a bandage.

Quil chuckled at the encouragement that there would be more times. "*Gut.* Because I don't know the scenic route."

"Remind me to give it to you for next time. There's a scenic overlook that might be *gut* for sparking."

Paris made some sort of noise he couldn't identify. But if she blushed any more, she'd be in danger of turning permanently pink. His face heated, too.

Quil took *Daadi*'s cup to him, then returned, and leaned against the doorjamb. He took a sip of the hot drink.

But a sparking place? That would be *gut* information to know.

❄

Paris had to get this matchmaking business out of *Mammi* Phoebe's head. She took it to unheard-of levels. *Jah,* she might be well aware of Paris's unrequited crush on Quil from years ago, but it didn't mean a thing now. As he'd said himself, he was on the rebound. And while she might've been desperate for any scrap of attention she could get back then, she wasn't the same girl anymore. She'd grown up.

Moved on.

Or at least tried to move on.

Because the Quil here in the room *noticed* her this time. And it stirred to life long-dormant feelings and emotions and made her want to twirl and turn cartwheels. Happy Birthday indeed. First the treats in town, the dress, the trip, the party, and then her very first kiss.

Mammi Phoebe stood, scooted her chair under the table, and turned. "Okay, finish your drink, dry your feet, and you'll be ready to go. I'll loan you a pair of socks because yours are soaked. I don't have any shoes that'll fit you, though. Maybe Quil will be kind enough to carry you to the buggy, and then up on your porch when you get home."

Paris sucked in a breath. "*Mammi* Phoebe, *nein.*" She simply couldn't bear to be in Quil's arms. Not now.

Quil winked. "I'd be glad to. We don't want you getting frostbite."

"I'm not a pampered princess. I can walk." Paris set her jaw, grabbed the towel *Mammi* Phoebe had placed on her lap, and busily dried her feet.

"I'll fetch a pair of socks." *Mammi* Phoebe turned away. "Aquila, remember what your *daed* used to say, 'Make hay while the sun shines.' That applies here, too."

"Yes, ma'am," Quil said in *Englisch.*

"Don't get impertinent with me, young man."

He winked at Paris. Again. He must've drained his hot cocoa, because he'd put his empty mug by the sink and crossed the room to lift Paris's coat off the hook. Someone must've brought over her bonnet and gloves, because he retrieved them from the top of a small cabinet near the door.

"Here's a pair of socks. You can return them when you come back next week." *Mammi* Phoebe handed Paris a balled object. "Put them on and skedaddle. It's past my bedtime."

Paris shrugged, tugged the socks on, and stood. Quil stepped forward and held her damp coat out for her to slide into, waited for her to tie on the black bonnet and pull on the gloves, then scooped her up, and headed out the door.

She squealed and pounded his back. "Put me down."

Not exactly the way she'd dreamed of being carried. But he chuckled, so this was deliberate, probably to tease his *mammi.*

"Not like that, you goof." *Mammi* Phoebe followed them to the door. She swatted the towel Paris had discarded at his backend but missed.

Quil gently lowered her into the buggy. "I'll go back in and get your shoes." His gaze was heated, which warmed her more effectively than any heater. He turned and went back to the *haus*. *Mammi* Phoebe met him at the door with Paris's shoes and said something to him that Paris couldn't hear.

He laughed. And was still laughing when he returned to the buggy. He climbed in, clicked his tongue at the horse, and guided it out onto the road.

"What was so funny?" Paris asked.

Quil's mouth quirked. "She told me she expects a full account of our ride home, and I'd better make the kiss a doozy." He glanced at her. "I told her I never kiss and tell."

Paris shivered and not from the cold. She couldn't keep her gaze from dipping to his perfect lips. "Your *mammi* is incorrigible."

"That she is."

She angled a look at him. "You better start making up a story now then, because a kiss isn't happening."

He flashed a grin. "We'll see, Little Miss Birthday Girl. We'll see."

❄

Quil stopped the buggy in front of Paris's *haus*, even though he fully intended to carry her to the door. This time, correctly. The way Amos carried Sarah. But Paris had put on her shoes in the buggy, even though they must be wet, and it didn't take a genius to know she intended to get there on her own power.

He wouldn't argue. Instead, he ground tethered the horse and took her arm as she got out of the buggy. Held on to her as they climbed the icy steps.

She turned to face him at the door. "*Danki*, Quil. You've been beyond kind. I really appreciate everything from the gift, to picking me up, finding me in the woods, and now dropping me off."

"You can thank me better." He held his arms wide. "You promised me a hug."

"I don't think it was a promise." The strangled note was back in her voice.

He couldn't remember her exact words, but it had been a promise, right? He shrugged. "I think it was." He hoped he sounded somewhat positive, and she wouldn't focus on the "I think" part.

She made a sound he couldn't identify and stepped into his arms. He closed them around her as she wrapped her arms around his waist in a too-loose, too-casual hug. One that reminded him of the ones *Mammi* used to give him when he came home from school and she saw him on a regular basis.

Not at all satisfactory.

Quil tightened his arms around her, tucking her against him, and when she looked up, her eyes wide, lips parted, he took full advantage of the opportunity.

She sucked in a breath, stiffening for a brief moment, then with a sigh, she leaned into him, her lips softening under his. Welcoming him. She tasted of cinnamon. Smelled of vanilla. A *wunderbaar* combination. Her hand curled around his neck, her fingers threading into his hair, and he groaned, deepening the kiss.

She made an answering whimper, her other arm going around his neck, and she kissed him back with something akin to desperation.

Heaven. This was absolutely heaven.

Something that sounded like a door squeaking open vaguely registered.

Quil's hands slipped down her back. He pressed her closer against him.

A door banged shut, ruining the moment. Something creaked.

Quil slowly raised his head. He glanced around but didn't see anything in the dark shadows. They were still alone. "That was amazing. You are amazing." The back of his fingers trailed down her cheek. "Would you go on a walk with me tomorrow?"

With a sharp intake of breath, she stepped out of his arms. "I'm not… I won't—"

Don't say it. "You're not a fling. You could never be a fling." He couldn't keep the note of desperation from his voice.

"I can't—"

"Please."

"I…I can't." There was a sound that might've been a sob in her voice.

Had his kisses ruined everything? Regret washed over him. "Look, I'm…I'm sorry." Except he wasn't. He'd do it again, given the opportunity. "I…I didn't mean—"

A lantern flicked on behind her and slowly rose as he struggled to make sense of it. The light put her in the shadows but illuminated the person who'd joined them sometime during their embrace.

"I think it's time for you to go, Aquila Stutzman."

Her *daed.*

Chapter Ten

Three weeks later

It was still dark when Paris got into the buggy beside *Daed*. He clicked at the horse. Treasure trod toward the road, slowly, as if wondering why the silly humans wanted to go to town at zero-dark-thirty.

Excitement bubbled inside Paris, and it took every bit of effort to sit still. She'd been looking forward to this trip to New York for weeks. It would be the first time she left Michigan. What would New York be like?

More importantly, would Quil go with them? He'd said he would but held off on paying the money upfront because he wasn't sure if his *daadi* would be able to let him go with Christmas fast approaching.

Quil. A shiver worked through her. She glanced at *Daed* to make sure he hadn't noticed. She'd thought of little else since that fateful night when Quil kissed her. When *Daed* caught them on the porch and banished Quil. She expected a lecture in the morning, but Daed looked lost in thought at breakfast, and his smile had been bittersweet.

At first, Paris had tried to avoid Quil at his *mammi*'s *haus* by ducking her head and dashing into another room, ashamed of her behavior. She'd totally given him the wrong—make that the right—impression, but she should've controlled herself better. Not revealed her long-time crush on him.

For his part, Quil had been equally determined not to let her avoid him. He deliberately tracked her down and talked about some mundane topic, drawing her all-too-willingly into the conversation, and beginning the steps toward a relationship, sharing hopes, beliefs, and dreams. The thrill of discovery. But always around his grandparents. Built-in chaperones. Even if *Mammi* Phoebe kept dropping hints and blatantly gave him directions for the scenic route.

He'd shown up at Paris's home on the days she didn't work for his grandparents, carrying a Cherry Coke and offering it to her, greeting *Mamm,* then helping *Daed* with his chores.

There'd been no more kisses. Paris sighed.

Mamm had looked at her with a smile and speculation in her gaze. "That boy is smitten."

Smitten. Right. Even if he wasn't, she was. Totally. Completely. Her face warmed just thinking of it. She squirmed in the buggy seat, drawing *Daed's* attention. She was thankful the darkness hid her blush.

Daed had begun to call him *sohn.* Welcoming him into their lives.

Paris wished for a repeat performance of the birthday-goodnight kiss on the porch. Because this Quil who sought her out and made conversation in an effort to get to know her had completely won her heart.

But yet, he hadn't approached her at the two singings they'd attended after *the kiss*. He'd taken a step or two toward her, his gaze holding hers long enough to make her heart rate increase, but he immediately seemed to change his mind or was waylaid by someone. He hadn't taken any other girls home though. He came late, left early, and alone. Always alone. At least he wasn't taking other girls home. That would've broken her heart. Leaving alone gave credence to his earlier comments about not getting involved in a relationship on the rebound. And it explained his red-faced apology when he stumbled off the porch after *Daed* had interrupted their embrace. She hadn't been sure whom he apologized to. To *Daed*, because Quil kissed her, or to her because they'd been caught?

Or maybe he was trying but going about it the right way this time. Slowly. Carefully. Cautiously.

She couldn't wait to spend time with him on the trip to New York. A long four-day weekend in Quil's company. Of course, Sarah, Amos, Noah, Aric, and a few others would be there, plus the chaperones: Bishop Miah and his wife Katherine. The bishop usually didn't act as chaperone, but he said he'd always wanted to see Niagara Falls and made an exception in this case.

Amos and the others decided it was a *gut* time to go to New York despite it being so close to Christmas. Only a week. Most of the farm work had slowed, seasonal jobs had ended, and they had a lot more free time.

Except for Quil. He was busy—tree sales were in full swing.

Treasure's muffled hoofbeats echoed Paris's thudding heart as they approached Main Street. Would he be there?

Daed drove up to the shops where the van was supposed to meet them. Quil stood among the ones already gathered. Paris's face warmed despite the chill. The van hadn't yet arrived, and Agnes was outside the shop passing out candy samples and free *koffee* in disposable cups to the ones gathered.

Paris's heart pounded.

Daed leaned over and kissed her cheek. "Have fun, dear girl. Remember what the bishop said. A dream is half a prophecy. Maybe your dreams will start coming true."

A dream is half a prophecy.

Even half a prophecy would be a dream come true.

If *Gott* smiled on her.

"Danki, Daed. I'll tell you all about it. And I'll take pictures, if I can." Paris climbed out of the buggy.

Agnes wrapped her in a hug. "I made a cup of hot chocolate for you because you don't like *koffee.*"

"Danki. That's really sweet of you." Paris returned the embrace.

"It's back at the shop. Leave your bag here with the others and come get it. But you need to hurry. I see the van." She pointed.

"Aren't you coming with us?" Paris dropped her bag in the pile of other luggage and hurried after Agnes.

"Nein. I have to stay and run the shop. I'm responsible for myself these days." Sadness colored Agnes's voice. "Besides, I might have other plans." The frown turned into a slight smile as she handed her a warm cup, gave her another quick hug, then ushered her out the door. "Go on now."

Paris hurried back to the others and slowed her steps. *Sarah.* There she was, lingering close to Quil. Would she flirt with him the entire trip? She'd heard someone was courting Sarah, though, but they hadn't talked since Paris's birthday. The way Sarah had treated her that day still stung.

Quil loaded Paris's bag in the back of the van, then turned to her with a smile. "They brought pop for the trip. It's in the cooler. I told them what you drink, so there are a few Cherry Cokes in there." He blushed. "And um, by the way, I might be ready."

"For what?" Paris glanced at Sarah who hesitated, before walking off to talk to someone else who'd just arrived.

He pointed to her, back to him, and then did it again. "You. Me. Us."

"Us?" Did he mean he wanted to court her? That he was over Priscilla and no longer worried about beginning a relationship on the rebound? She frowned, trying to decipher his three one-word answers.

"Jah. Us." He licked his lips. "They're, uh, loading up. We'll talk later. You'd best go find a seat. Save one for me. Next to you."

Paris found a seat in the back row with Arie and Noah with

room for Quil in case he was serious. Sarah and Amos sat in the row ahead of them, while Bishop Miah sat up front with the driver, directing traffic and giving orders. Was Amos the one courting Sarah? Maybe she should try to talk to her friend. They used to share all their secrets… and now, she knew nothing. Paris missed their long, giggly conversations. Missed having a best friend.

Though, Arie had been friendly and might step into that vacancy.

"Did everyone remember their passports?" Amos stood and waved his. "Make sure it's handy. You're going to need it when we cross the bridge into Canada."

Paris checked her purse. It was tucked inside.

"Gut," Amos said after everyone verified they had theirs. "In about eight hours we'll see the Canadian side of Niagara Falls."

This was going to be such an adventure. And she was sharing it with Quil.

He loaded the last bag into the storage area and climbed in. Quil's gaze met Paris's and without hesitating, he made a beeline for the back of the van and settled beside her. She scooted closer to Arie, leaving room between her and the window. A few others, Mose Graber, his sister, Liz, and a male cousin of his that Paris didn't know, took the last few seats.

Her heart rate increased as Quil's piney scent wafted over her. His leg pressed against hers in the narrow confines of the bench seat. He leaned over and said something to Noah on the far side of Arie, but his words were drowned as the engine roared to life, the radio blasted, and the bishop shouted last minute instructions to whoever could actually hear him. Or whoever was actually trying to listen.

Quil leaned back, rested an arm around the back of the seat, and curved it around Paris's shoulders. "Feel free to use me as a pillow," he whispered.

Paris's face heated.

Noah did the same with Arie, wrapping her in a loose hug. It made it a little easier, even though most of the *youngies* on the van had paired off. Noah and Arie. Amos and Sarah. When had that happened? Sarah could've told Paris. Some best friend Sarah was.

Paris smiled. It didn't matter, because now she was part of a couple, too. If Quil's confusing *"You. Me. Us."* comment meant what she thought it did.

She settled into his embrace and hoped the bishop and his wife didn't see her snuggling against him.

Paris and Quil. At long last.

A dream come true.

Either that, or it was a heartache in the making.

The jury was still out.

❄

The parking lot on the Canadian side of the falls was almost empty, probably because it was off-season. They disembarked and made their way out to the observation deck. The falls were lit by beautiful multicolored lights and made a terrible roar. With his gloved hands, Quil grasped the top of the fence and gazed in wonder. *Wow.* He'd never imagined he'd be able to see such a sight. The mist from the falls drifted his direction and added to the chill but being here with Paris beside him warmed him up.

"There is something mesmerizing and soothing about watching those torrents of water rush to who knows where." Paris snapped a picture with her cell phone. "*Mamm* and *Daed* will want to see this."

He nodded. "Show it to *Mammi* and *Daadi,* too. *Gott* is truly an awesome *Gott.* Not only imagining all this but creating it."

"Creating the whole universe." She leaned over the rail with a sigh of contentment. "I could watch this all night." She slipped the phone back into her purse and put on her gloves.

Quil glanced behind him, catching Sarah's glare aimed at Paris.

Hopefully, Paris wouldn't notice. The bishop waved to get his attention, then motioned for him to come. Quil gave a nod of acknowledgment. "I'll buy you a postcard or two. I think they want to get dinner and find a hotel."

"Oh." Sighing, Paris gave a last lingering look at the falls. "At least we'll see this again before we leave."

"I'll bring you back for our honeymoon." That should make his intentions clear.

Paris's eyes widened, and her lips parted. "Are you—?"

He shook his head and winked. "Come on."

Quil stayed as close to Paris as possible, not touching her, though he wanted to grasp her hand and hold on tight. The bishop and his wife hadn't said anything about Paris dozing on his shoulder during the long van ride, but public displays of affection were frowned upon. They even walked about a foot apart. That didn't stop Sarah from casting hateful looks their way.

Quil gave her a pointed look and a head-tilt toward Amos. If that didn't work, he probably should consider warning his new friend about her fickle ways.

Despite the temperatures hovering near freezing, they rode the *Maid of the Mist*. Quil stood beside Paris in the long line to ride the elevator from the top to the bottom. They put on bright yellow hooded raincoats that covered Paris all the way to her ankles. His ended below his knees. Some of the tourists stayed under the boat's canopy so they wouldn't get wet from the freezing cold spray, but Quil, Paris, Noah, Arie, and Amos went out on the deck. Sarah refused, and it was no wonder. He'd been visiting last winter when the girls fell through the thin ice pond. That experience would make anyone paranoid of cold water.

It was amazing standing so close to Niagara Falls, to reach out his hand and embrace the mist falling on and around him.

Quil glanced down at Paris. Her lips parted as she laughed, arms outstretched, twirling on the boat's deck. He wanted to catch her to him, hug her tightly, and steal a kiss. Someday—*jah,* someday—he'd kiss her in the rain.

Better yet, he'd kiss her while standing in the spray from Niagara Falls. He couldn't think of anything more romantic.

But Quil had promised her *daed* he wouldn't do anything inappropriate on this trip during the parental lecture that came on the heels of the what-are-your-intentions-toward-my-daughter discussion. Her *daed* meant business. Quil and Paris were together as part of a group, not as a couple. Not yet.

After they disembarked *Maid of the Mist,* they went to Cave of the Winds. It was cold, and the different bright yellow hooded raincoat issued to him there got beyond drenched, but it was well worth it. He could go right up to where the water hit him coming down. Quil tried to stay close to Paris. He wanted to feel her joy, and wished he'd put that huge smile on her face as she stood, arms raised high and wide, as the water flowed over her. He would've hugged her close and kissed her senseless if they were alone.

That evening, after visiting the aquarium, they walked out to the observation deck between Rainbow and Bridal Veil Falls. He gazed at the view, trying to commit it to memory. It was so beautiful. Paris snapped more pictures. Quil didn't want this vacation to end or to ever forget this time with Paris. If only he could capture her expression on film. Another thing to memorize. Her wide-eyed excitement filled him with joy.

This trip was a treasure trove of memories, but she was *the* treasure.

❄

The trip to New York State was passing way too fast. Paris didn't want it to end, but at the same time, she was eager to share it with her parents, to record it in her diary. And maybe, if what Quil indicated were true to spend their honeymoon here. To have Quil —the man of her longtime dreams—court her.

Her!

She'd figured she wasn't *gut* enough for Quil.

Sarah sure didn't think she was, if her hateful glares were any indication. It was hard to ignore them, and any attempts Paris made to talk were rebuffed by Sarah pointedly turning her back, as if shunning Paris.

She tied her black bonnet on over her prayer *kapp* and glanced around the cluttered motel room she shared with Arie, Sarah, and Liz. Her last full day here. She intended to spend the whole day beside Quil. Maybe he'd touch her, find a quiet secluded alley and steal a kiss, or something. A delicious chill worked through her. She couldn't control her shiver.

"You're making a fool out of yourself." Sarah glared at Paris from where she stood by the door, shrugging her coat on. "Twirling in the waterfall mist, and later, laughing at those sea animals just to get Quil's attention. You should be ashamed. You're just like your real mother. You'll never be *gut* enough for him. He'll marry a sensible Amish girl like Liz. I'm possibly out of the picture, because Amos asked to court me."

"I thought we were friends. Why are you acting like this?" Paris immediately wished the words back. She sounded childish.

"I am your friend." Sarah pursed her lips. "Friends don't let friends make fools of themselves. And your behavior is despicable."

Was that what she was doing? Making a fool out of herself? Paris's eyes burned. She sucked in a breath and bit her lip, trying to control her emotions. She couldn't show Sarah how much her words hurt.

Paris glanced at Liz, who hadn't said more than two words during the entire trip. Even now she wordlessly twisted her hair up and pinned it then secured her *kapp* over it, eyes downcast as if afraid to look at the others.

Liz wasn't Quil's type.

Paris marveled that she'd even caught his eye. She was nothing like beautiful, curvy Priscilla.

"What are you talking about, Sarah?" Arie frowned. She took a step closer to Paris. "She's not—"

Sarah tossed her head and gave Paris a triumphant smirk. "She was adopted out of the *Englisch* foster care system. My aunt told me all about her when I complained about Paris's actions on her birthday. She heard that Paris's real *mamm* was a prostitute. That's the kind of girl hanging out with us. It's actually amazing the Amish allowed her to fellowship with us."

"What! My birth *mamm* was *what*?" Paris wanted to collapse in a ball on the bed, cover her face with a pillow, and disappear. Her legs weakened. She lifted her chin and tried to pretend it didn't matter. But was Sarah telling the truth? Paris had known she was adopted out of the foster care system, but her parents hadn't told her why except that her real *mamm* couldn't take care of her.

Liz managed to slip into the bathroom and shut the door, casting a worried glance toward Sarah as if she expected the next attack.

Arie took another step closer to Paris. "I'm sure—"

"The apple doesn't fall far from the parental tree." Sarah aimed another smirk at Paris. "She'll become just like her real mother, a prostitute. Besides, *Gott* punishes the children for the sin of the parents to the third and fourth generation. She's cursed. And all that awfulness is coming out on this trip, the way she's shamelessly flirting with Quil."

Arie gasped. Her hand rose to cover her heart, and she shook her head.

Paris blinked at the burn in her eyes. There went her friendship with Arie. She pressed her fingers against her lips. It wouldn't do any *gut* to deny it, not when she didn't know the true story.

"Enough." Arie's hand made a slashing movement. "How unkind, Sarah. We shouldn't gossip like this. Besides, Paris is fine." She glanced toward Paris. "I'm excited about this trip, too. I hate that it's ending so soon. Besides, if she was acting inappropriately, the bishop would've said something."

Paris wanted to hug her. She was glad for her new friendship with Arie and that, with Quil and Noah in the picture, they'd been drifting together more. She didn't need Sarah's negativity. If only they were jealousy-based lies. But she had no way of knowing. She needed to get out of this room with her dignity intact and try to enjoy the rest of her birthday gift trip. She moved toward the door to leave.

"You're acting like an overly excited child, not a young woman old enough to marry." Sarah ignored Arie and focused on Paris. "I'm going to tell the bishop. And after your shocking behavior on your birthday, I'm surprised he didn't make you kneel and confess for that."

The bishop hadn't said a word to Paris about her birthday. Other than a whispered "a merry heart does *gut* like medicine" when he came to visit with *Daed*. At the time, it'd seemed like one of his random, seemingly meaningless comments, but now, weeks later, it'd begun to make sense, even if his other comment about *ask, seek, knock* still puzzled her. Maybe someday that'd be clear. At least he hadn't condemned her. That gave her a bit of inner peace.

She turned her back to Sarah and rolled her eyes.

Arie gave an answering eye roll.

Paris mouthed, "*Danki*," and with Arie's nod, she firmed her shoulders and tried to shrug off the lingering effect of Sarah's tirade, so she could go on to enjoy her day.

"I sure hope you behave yourself today, though I really think it's inappropriate to visit an old Army fort. And a whirlpool. Who cares about staring at swirling water anyway?" Sarah asked.

Arie reached for her coat. "The whirlpool in Niagara River is supposed to be a tourist attraction. I'm excited to see it."

"*Jah*, but people drown in it, like all the time." Sarah shuddered. "I'm not going to get too close."

Paris wanted to hike to see the whirlpool, but she didn't want to get too near. It did sound dangerous.

Someone pounded on the door. "You all ready to go?"

Sarah pulled it open. "We're just finishing up. Can't wait." She beamed at Amos.

Liz came out of the bathroom and reached for her coat.

Paris rubbed her throbbing head. She didn't want a tension headache today, but like it or not, she had one. Hopefully, it wouldn't turn into a migraine. She picked up her coat and followed the others out of the room.

"You don't look very *gut.*" Quil sat beside her on the drive out to Fort Niagara. "Are you okay?"

Paris forced a smile. "Tension headache." No way would she share the truth of it. He'd probably judge her as harshly as Sarah had. Except, Arie had heard it—and accepted it. Accepted her.

With a frown, he glanced around, then quickly leaned in and planted a gentle kiss on her temple. "I'll pray you feel better soon."

Just having his cool lips touch her temple helped. A little. But not her roiling stomach. Sarah would probably share the horrible truth with Quil, and then their fledgling relationship would be over—unless he reacted as Arie did. But then again, friendship and courting were two different things. That might make a difference.

On the other hand, most of the Amish knew she was adopted out of the foster care system. Did they whisper about her behind her back? Quil wouldn't even have to hear it from Sarah. His own *mammi* probably knew the truth. Paris needed to ask *Mamm* and *Daed* about her past.

Her stomach knotted and churned hard enough to put to shame the whirlpool they were about to see.

Because the Niagara River and the whirlpool were very close to Fort Niagara, they went there first. Thankful for a true friend who stuck by her, Paris hiked with Arie through the fort, snapping pictures, then found the others. Noah studied an old cannon standing guard outside the fort. "I wonder how they shot these things. They're nothing like the rifles we use for deer hunting."

"I'm going to hike down to the whirlpool," Quil said.

"I'm not going anywhere near it." Sarah pursed her lips. "I'll wait in the van."

"Aw, come on. You'll regret not seeing it." Amos smiled at her. "You don't need to get close enough to fall in."

Paris didn't wait for Sarah to decide. She joined Quil and the others as they walked the trail to the river and climbed over large rocks.

The water was frightening in its intensity. Paris didn't want to get too close to it herself. She stayed back as the men got as close as they could, but she gave her cell phone to Quil, so he could take a picture.

Then they walked side-by-side back to the van where Sarah stubbornly waited.

The headache eased as the happy day unfolded into a great evening of fireworks over the falls. The only nagging irritation had been the glares Sarah still shot at Paris behind everyone's back, followed by an awful contemplative smirk as they walked back to the van.

As they were getting off the van at the hotel, Sarah pulled Quil aside and glared at Paris. "I think there's something you need to know."

Chapter Eleven

Paris stumbled and grabbed hold of Arie's upper arm in an effort to keep her balance.

Arie stared at Paris as if horns had sprouted through her *kapp*.

Paris swallowed the bile rising in her throat. Should she pretend she didn't hear Sarah's comment to Quil, pretend she didn't know the implications behind the glare, pretend she didn't care? Or should she demand Sarah say what she intended in front of her? See firsthand Quil's reaction when he discovered the horrid truth of her parentage, if what Sarah said was true? She didn't remember her life before *Mamm* and *Daed* adopted her. But someone did—or thought they did—and had gossiped about Paris, spreading horrible stories. Sarah's earlier words now fueled the feeling of being unworthy to be accepted as Amish, unworthy of being loved, unworthy of Quil. Unworthy, even of *Gott*.

How could she manage to hold her head up again?

She stood there beside the van, gripping Arie's arm, and looking like a silly fool. *Go, or stay*. Her stomach churned, while all but Mose and his cousin Timothy waited beside the van.

Paris pried her fingers loose from Arie's arm and balled her fists. Arie rubbed her upper arm. Paris would need to apologize for any bruises later. She forced a smile—that probably resembled a grimace—and faced Sarah head on. "If you're talking about me, say it to my face." It couldn't be any worse than what she'd said in the hotel room.

Somebody gasped. Paris didn't see who it was, but she supposed her behavior was shocking. Confrontational. Maybe even prideful, as if she believed that, of course, it would be all about her.

Though the glare Sarah leveled at her, combined with her unkind words before they left the hotel room, strongly indicated it was.

Arie moved closer to her.

Sarah's face flamed red. She looked toward the bishop and his wife, who still stood with the others. Bishop Miah's brow rose. "I didn't mean now. I meant I'll talk to him later."

"If it's about Paris, whatever it is you think I need to know should come from her, not you." Quil glanced at Sarah, then Paris. "I don't listen to gossip."

"It's not gossip. It's the truth," Sarah protested.

"Then she can tell me herself, if she wants me to know." Quil winked at Paris and strode toward the hotel with Noah at his side. Amos and Liz followed.

Relief filled Paris. Quil didn't want to hear anything from Sarah. Their possible courting relationship wasn't over yet. Her secret was still safe for a while. And his wink sent delightful shivers up her spine.

Bishop Miah and Katherine hovered by the van, eyeing Paris and Sarah. Did they expect a fight to break out?

Arie put her arm around Paris's shoulder. "Come on. Let's go in. Maybe we can get something to drink and go someplace quiet to talk."

Paris nodded. Would Arie know what she had done to alienate the woman she'd formerly considered her best friend? She didn't have a clue, but maybe Arie would. She walked to the hotel. It would be nice to find a quiet table and have ice cream. Much better than a drink. An entire quart with two spoons. But since that wasn't an option, she'd settle for an ice cream cone.

"Ice cream sounds better. Do you want to walk to McDonalds?" Paris pointed to the golden arches down the street.

Arie glanced at the bishop.

He nodded. "*Jah,* that sounds *gut.*"

Arie smiled. Paris relaxed at the kind tone of his voice.

"We'll tell Noah and Quil," Katherine said.

"Tell them to give us a thirty-minute head start." Arie hooked her arm with Paris's. "We need to talk before they arrive."

Except Paris's stomach still churned. Couldn't she just drown her sorrows in ice cream and skip the talk?

"Come on." Arie tugged Paris toward the road. "I can't believe her aunt shared that nonsense with her. You were an innocent child who had nothing to say about your parents' decisions. If that story is even true." She raised her eyebrows.

Paris shook her head. "I don't know. I'd love to have a reason to hope it might not be."

"There are always elements of truth in rumors, but they usually aren't the whole truth," Arie said. "I think your parents did a *wunderbaar* thing, adopting you from the foster care system. I've known others who were adopted."

Paris shrugged. "I wish I wasn't adopted. That I really was a Kauffman. Either that or my birth *mamm* would've loved me enough to want me and take care of me, instead of giving me away."

"I'm not sure, but I think you have to be neglected or abused to get into the foster care system. I might be wrong, though. Assuming what Sarah said is true, you'd rather live as your real *mamm* did instead of having your current life?" Arie's eyes widened.

Paris's shoulders sagged. "I didn't mean that. I meant… I don't know what I meant."

"May I tell you a story?"

"Sure. A story is fine." Maybe it'd help to take her mind off herself.

Arie slowed her walk as they neared the fast food restaurant. "In the spring, when the flowers came up, one of the marigold seeds we'd planted came up in the driveway, not in the garden. I went out there and dug up the plant and transplanted it into the flowerbed. Not because it wasn't valuable to us, but because it would die where it was planted. It wouldn't thrive. What if *Gott* saw you planted in the wrong environment, and He wanted you to grow and thrive so He transplanted you?"

Paris furrowed her brow. Arie had given her some food for thought. "I love my life. I can't imagine not being who I am. My parents love me. I have brothers and sisters who love me. Grandparents, aunts, uncles, and cousins. I just wish I deserved the love of *my* family. That I deserved my friends." Though, maybe Sarah was the type of friend she deserved. She frowned, her eyes burning. "I wish I deserved *Gott*'s love. And Quil. But he'll run the opposite direction when he finds out."

"I daresay he already knows. And the other flowers don't reject one that's transplanted. They welcome it. It's the weeds that try to choke out the *gut* plants. You don't need weedy friends." Arie pulled open the glass door to the fast food restaurant and let go of Paris's arm. "Order what you want. My treat."

"*Danki.*" Paris got into line. "It really is too bad McDonalds doesn't sell ice cream in quart boxes. But—"

"Jenny, eggnog milkshake." A server plopped a clear plastic cup on the counter.

Paris approached the counter as a customer lifted the milkshake from the counter.

A milkshake was ice cream, right? And it'd be a larger serving than a soft cone. Even better, it came in chocolate. That'd be enough to fix everything. Almost. Okay, maybe not even remotely. At least it'd make her feel a little better for a few minutes.

"Are you ready to order?" The server glanced at Paris.

Paris gave her order, and Arie ordered a hot cappuccino, then handed the server enough cash for both. When they got their drinks, Arie led the way to an empty corner of the restaurant. A small round table that was raised higher than usual with high chairs.

"You think Quil already knows?" As soon as they were seated, Paris brought up the previous topic, her voice strangled. Then her face heated.

"There are few secrets among the Amish. Pretty much everyone knows everything about everyone."

That was true. The Amish always seemed to know who was related to whom and when so-and-so's relative from such-and-such was coming for a visit, or even rumors that someone was courting someone else. The rumor mill was usually accurate.

"No one cares you were adopted except Sarah. She's jealous of you. Why do you think she was so quick to claim you were her best friend when you moved here? It was so she could hang out with you and enjoy everything you did. She used you."

"What?" Paris caught her breath.

Arie smiled. "You are so sweet. Everyone knows it. You really shouldn't let her bother you."

Easier said than done. Paris wiggled the straw around in the milkshake, then fished the cherry off the top, and popped it in her mouth.

The chair next to her swiveled as Bishop Miah eased himself on it. "This isn't so easy on my hips. I had an awful time trying to catch up with you two. By the time I got the message to Quil and Noah, you two were already halfway here." He slid a five-dollar bill toward Arie. "Get me a *koffee,* with cream and sugar, and a fried pie, please. And don't tell Katherine. She'll have my hide."

Paris giggled.

Arie took the money and slid off the stool. "She'll know by bedtime, whether we tell her or not."

The bishop chuckled. "She likely will, because I'll confess." He waited until Arie walked off, before leaning toward Paris. "Katherine stayed to have a talk with Sarah and Liz about what happened, but we'll probably not get one word of explanation from Liz, and Sarah's story will be skewed, so I want to hear your side."

Paris didn't know where to start. She sighed as she stirred the milkshake again. Then she took a sip, getting a mouthful of whipped cream as she tried to formulate how to begin.

The bishop sighed. "I understand you don't want to say anything against Sarah. But you should know she didn't hesitate to come to me with wild stories about your birthday treasure hunt. She said you were shamelessly flirting with Quil."

Paris blinked back tears. *Sarah* was shamelessly flirting with Quil. Not Paris.

"She also said you were soaking up undeserved adulation from everyone in the community. But it was your birthday, and people usually want to celebrate. Though, that might be part of Sarah's problem. Her family doesn't celebrate birthdays. Her jealousy might be understood there."

Paris nodded, frowning. A tear escaped. She brushed it away.

Bishop Miah drummed his fingers on the table. "But this trip? She's here, and I've heard Amos is courting her." He frowned and shook his head. "I always thought Liz would be a better choice for him." The finger thumping increased.

Paris had nothing to say to that random rabbit trail either. She wiped another tear away and took a sip of her milkshake. A mix of whipped cream and chocolate.

"Ah-ha!" He slapped the table, making Paris jump. "A bird in hand is worth two in the bush, but she really wants one of the birds that's still in the bush."

What? Paris tried to decipher that. Was she supposed to say something to the birds and bushes tangent? Her mind spun.

The bishop smacked the table again. "So, now that we've figured Sarah out, back to you. What is your side of the story?"

Her turn. And she still didn't know where to begin. She didn't want to have an emotional dump on Bishop Miah's shoulders.

Arie set a tray containing an apple pie, a *koffee,* and a few coins down in front of the bishop. "Sarah shared gossip about Paris's past. She said her aunt told her Paris is the daughter of a prostitute, and Paris is just like her birth mother. So now Paris feels she doesn't deserve her family's love, Quil's attention, or God's love, either."

"Pure supposition." Bishop Miah waved it away as if it was nonsense.

With a soft smile, Arie sat in her chair and took of sip of her cappuccino.

He turned to pierce Paris with a fierce gaze as if drilling this truth into her doubting skull. "All I know from talking to your parents when they first moved to the area is that you were placed in foster care because your birth mother could no longer take care of you. There are so many reasons why a child might be put into foster care and kept there until released for adoption. And your foster parents were quick to claim you when you were available. But whatever the case, you had no say in the circumstances of your birth, or in your parents' decisions."

The knot in Paris's stomach started to ease.

"You only have a say in the choices you make. And as for deserving..." Bishop Miah shook his head. "None of us deserve *Gott*'s grace. We deserve to die as Christ Jesus did. But because of His great mercy, He sent His son to die in your stead. You are a treasure to God."

Paris stirred her milkshake again. Then took another sip. This time she got a mouthful of chocolate. It tasted *gut* and helped her emotions as much as this conversation did.

"He sent His only son to be born as a baby and to die for your sins on the cross. He bought you with a great price. He loves you and wants you to run to Him with your cares and concerns."

Gott loved her that much? She smiled. *Danki, Lord, for your great gift to us. To me.*

"I shall have a long chat with Sarah when we get home. I'll make sure her parents are involved. I wouldn't worry about her, Paris. You are valuable as you are, you have friends and family who love you, and who knows? You might be a princess."

Arie smiled big and reached for Paris's hand. "I love that."

"I know for a fact that you're somebody's princess." Bishop Miah took a sip of his *koffee.*

The door burst open, letting in a blast of cold air, and Quil and Noah strode to the table.

"Not sure half an hour passed yet, boys." The bishop pretended to frown.

Paris giggled with a lighter heart.

Quil grinned. "Close enough. What's going on?"

Bishop Miah gathered his things and stood. "I'll be right over there, if you need me, but for now, I'll leave you to talk."

❄

Quil settled into the seat the bishop had vacated as Arie and Noah moved to another table closer to the bishop. Quil reached for Paris's hand, entwining their fingers. "This trip was amazing. I'm so glad I was able to come. The only bad part was Sarah." He frowned, his fingers tightening around hers. "I don't want her to gossip about you."

Tears filled Paris's eyes. If only he could pull her into his arms and comfort her. "She was going to tell you I was adopted out of the foster care system."

"I know. I remember you were a foster child when we were in the early years of school together because you were still struggling to learn the language. I didn't know you were adopted until you told me your last name on your birthday. So I asked *Mammi.* She scolded me for not paying attention to what was right under my nose." He smiled. "But she told me the story anyway."

"Sarah was also going to tell you horrible stories about my birth *mamm.* I don't know if it is true or not."

"It doesn't matter what she was going to say. It won't change anything. I know the truth."

"What is the truth?" Her voice broke.

Quil rubbed his thumb over the back of her hand. "*Mammi* said that your birth *mamm* had been an exchange student in France. She came home pregnant, and she wanted to keep you. But she was in a car accident and died when you were two. You were placed in the foster care system until they could find any next of kin who'd take you. The father couldn't or wouldn't take you, and your birth mom's parents had disowned her and you. So you were released for adoption."

"Is that true?" Paris's eyes widened. "Or is that just a story she made up?" But that might explain her name.

Quil shrugged. "I've never heard *Mammi* tell a lie, so it must be true."

"The bishop would say it's supposition." Paris smiled.

"She was your parents' neighbor in Mio, so I'm guessing she knows more than most."

Paris grinned. "I could kiss you for that."

Quil chuckled, and his hand tightened around hers. "I'll hold you to that. But someplace less public than your back porch. I'd hate to be interrupted again." His gaze lowered.

Paris blushed and took another sip of her chocolate shake.

"When we get home, may I court you?" Quil hadn't intended to ask her here. The words just slipped out. But he wouldn't wish them back.

Paris's smile grew. "This is the best Christmas season ever. You came into my life, I learned the truth about my past, I found new friends, and it's all wrapped up and tied in a beautiful bow with Jesus's birth, death, and resurrection."

"All wrapped up and tied in a beautiful bow." He squeezed her hand as something warmed in his chest. He dipped his head. "*Danki,* Father, for Your loving gift to us this season. You've given us a great treasure. Help us to love You and serve You with all that we are. In Jesus's name, Amen."

He looked up into the glowing warmth of Paris's sweet eyes in response to his prayer.

"Amen," she whispered.

Then he leaned over, ignoring anyone who might be watching, and brushed his lips over Paris's.

"I love you. And I'm so thankful *Gott* opened my eyes to the treasure of you."

The end.

Coconut Potato Fudge Recipe

Ingredients:

- 1/2 cup plain, mashed potatoes, either instant or one medium potato, cooked
- 1/8 cup finely chopped (or crushed) almonds (optional)
- 3 cups powdered sugar
- 1 cup shredded coconut
- 1 teaspoon pure vanilla extract
- 3 ounces semi sweet baking chocolate
- 3 tablespoons butter

Instructions:

1. Beat powdered sugar and coconut into warm potatoes; then add the vanilla extract and almonds.
2. Press into a lightly-greased 8-inch square pan; set aside.
3. In a saucepan over low heat, melt chocolate and butter, stirring occasionally. When melted, pour over top of the potato mixture.
4. Refrigerate until set and then cut into squares.
5. Store in an airtight container in the refrigerator.

About the Author

Laura V. Hilton is an award-winning, sought-after author with almost twenty Amish, contemporary, and historical romances. When she's not writing, she reviews books for her blogs, and writes devotionals for blog posts for Seriously Write and Putting on the New.

Laura and her pastor-husband have five children and a hyper dog named Skye. They currently live in Arkansas. One son is in the U.S. Coast Guard. She is a pastor's wife, and homeschools her two youngest children.

When she's not writing, Laura enjoys reading, and visiting lighthouses and waterfalls. Her favorite season is winter, her favorite holiday is Christmas.

MISTLETOE AND MIRACLES

By Rachel J. Good

Chapter One

Daniel Graber whistled a cheerful tune as brisk November winds practically pushed him through the door of the Fairview Rehab Center. He greeted the staff at the desk and then made his way to *Daed*'s room.

When the door squeaked open, Daniel winced.

Before he could apologize, *Daed*'s voice boomed into the hallway. "Can't a man get any peace? I close my eyes for a nap and just manage to fall asleep. Then that horrible squeal wakes me up."

"Sorry, *Daed*," Daniel said, peeking into the room. He'd prayed for patience, and it seemed he would need it again today.

"Oh, it's you. Thought it was that girl who comes in here to make me do those exercises."

"I hope you're cooperating." But Daniel had a feeling he knew the answer.

With a loud huff, *Daed* screwed his face into a scowl. "I don't see how putting myself through pain will help me recover faster."

Daniel sighed, more to himself than aloud. The minute he walked through the door of his father's room at the rehab center each day, *Daed*'s querulous complaints and demands began.

Unfortunately, *Daed* still had four more weeks of physical therapy and rehab care.

Daed groused about the food—every meal Daniel shared was delicious. *Daed* disliked the staff—Daniel found all the workers—both Amish and Mennonite—were cheerful and kind. *Daed* griped about his roommate—the cheerful *Englisch* man in the other bed had gone home a few days ago, but that hadn't stopped *Daed*'s criticism. So far, the rehab center hadn't given *Daed* a new roommate, and Daniel wondered if the staff had chosen to leave the other bed empty to decrease some of *Daed*'s complaints. Or maybe they wanted to protect other residents from a steady stream of negativity.

"I want you to take me home today," *Daed* demanded.

Perhaps *Daed*'s grumpiness was an attempt to get out of the rehab center, or maybe his grouchiness came from being in constant pain. Daniel tried not to let his exasperation show. "Even if I could take you home, you'd still be confined to bed," he pointed out. "Besides, the crops are all harvested now, so you aren't missing out on work."

The mutinous expression on *Daed*'s face indicated he was about to explode.

A light tap sounded at the door, and a pretty Amish woman stuck her head in. "I came to see if you were ready for physical therapy now." Her eyes widened when she caught sight of Daniel. "*Ach*, I'm sorry. I didn't realize you had company."

"It's all right," Daniel said. "I'm his son. I come every day, so it's no problem if he goes to physical therapy while I'm here."

"If you don't mind?" She raised a questioning eyebrow. "I came to take him earlier, but he was asleep, so I rescheduled his appointment."

Daniel suspected *Daed* had been feigning sleep earlier, and he didn't want his father giving this sweet aide any trouble. "Would it be all right if I come along?"

"Of course." She beamed at him. "I'm sure the physical therapist wouldn't mind."

Daed's glower made it clear he wasn't happy with Daniel's maneuvering. "I don't—"

Daniel cut him off. "You wouldn't want to cause trouble for—" He paused and turned to the aide.

"Fern," she said, with a heart-stopping smile.

"Nice to meet you," Daniel managed after a dazed moment. He turned back to *Daed*. "You wouldn't want to make Fern's job difficult, would you?"

Pinching his lips into a straight line, *Daed* shot Daniel an exasperated look. "It hurts." This time his voice came out more plaintive than grumbly.

"I'm so sorry, Moses," Fern said. "I wish I could take away the pain."

Daed blinked several times and seemed to be as charmed by Fern as Daniel. "Maybe if you stayed with me," *Daed* told her, "it would help."

Fern reached for the wheelchair she'd parked in the hallway and pushed it over to the bed. "I'd be happy to stay if I could, but they need me elsewhere."

Daniel stepped over to the bed and helped *Daed* into the wheelchair. Fern looked much too petite to bear *Daed*'s weight.

"*Danke*," she said shyly. "You didn't have to do that."

"Happy to help." *More than happy.* "I can push him," he offered.

Fern shook her head. "I'm getting paid to do this job. If other people handle it, they might decide they don't need me."

Daniel stepped back so she could get behind the wheelchair. "Sorry, I wasn't trying to make you lose your job." He sucked in a breath as Fern brushed past him, her black apron whispering against his trouser leg as she took her place. He forced himself to step back, but it didn't calm the crescendoing of his heart.

"Are you new?" *Daed* asked, his voice not nearly as sharp as it had been earlier.

"Yes, I am." Fern maneuvered the wheelchair expertly out the door and pivoted to the left. "Today's my first day. I only moved to the Ephrata area a week ago."

Had he detected a bit of sadness in her eyes? It flickered away so quickly, it might have been a flash of light. "Do you like it here?" Daniel asked.

"I'm just settling in, but so far everyone seems quite friendly." She pivoted the wheelchair and headed for the door.

Daniel followed. "I guess you came from the Midwest." Rather than the gauzy, heart-shaped white *kapp* of the Lancaster area, Fern wore the stiffer, more rounded shape from farther west.

"Charm, Ohio," she said, as she pushed *Daed* into the elevator.

"I hope you'll settle in well here." Daniel wouldn't mind getting to know her better. "By the way, I'm Daniel. Daniel Graber."

"Nice to meet you, Daniel," she said politely.

He wished she'd shake his hand, but she disappointed him by gripping the wheelchair handles tightly. Stepping to a spot where he could study her without her noticing, Daniel barely paid attention to his stomach dropping as the elevator descended. Usually, that whooshing bothered him, but today he was too busy appreciating the gentle slope of Fern's nose, the pink blush of her cheek, and the black sweep of her eyelashes.

When the elevator shuddered to a stop, Daniel jerked his gaze back to *Daed*'s wheelchair. But even there, the small, pretty hands wrapped around the handles arrested his attention.

"Right this way," Fern said after the doors opened, and Daniel followed willingly.

He opened the door to the physical therapy room for her and stayed close as Fern spoke with the physical therapist. Because, of course, he should stay informed about *Daed*'s health, not because he was fascinated by the new aide.

❄

Fern clutched the wheelchair handles so tightly her fingers ached, and she tried to have a coherent conversation with the physical therapist while Daniel Graber hovered near her shoulder. Most likely he was concerned about his *daed*, but with him so near his breath whispered in her hair—or maybe she only imagined that—she struggled to keep her composure.

"This is Moses Graber," she said to Debbie. "I switched his ten o'clock appointment to now. He was asleep earlier."

Slight indentations deepened near the bridge of Debbie's nose. "Yes, I'm staying an extra half hour to accommodate him."

"*Ach*, I'm so sorry. I didn't mean to make extra work for you." Twice today, she'd upset the usual schedule by requesting changes for patients she'd been assigned to transport.

When Fern went into the rooms, she couldn't bring herself to wake anyone who was sleeping. Her heart went out to those who barely slept at night. Until recently, her *daed* had suffered...

Fern blinked away the tears that pooled in her eyes. But her *daed*'s insomnia, due to cancer and old age, made her compassionate if people snatched an hour or two of rest during the day.

So far, she'd already been lectured once. If Debbie complained, it might mean another reprimand. With two warnings on her first day, would she lose her job?

"Are you all right?" Daniel asked as the physical therapist took the wheelchair from her and pushed Moses over to the equipment.

"I'm not sure they'll keep me at this job. I tried to be helpful, to let your *daed* nap. I should have asked about Debbie's schedule. Now I've made her stay late." Fern wished she hadn't been the cause of that inconvenience. She clamped her teeth on her lower lip to avoid spilling any other worries.

Daniel shook his head. "I can't believe they'd get rid of someone for being kind."

"They already told me I need to stick to the appointment

schedules." Although she tried to sound matter-of-fact, her voice quavered.

"But aren't people more important than schedules?"

Fern warmed to him even more. "That's exactly how I feel." She shot him a smile. "But as my supervisor pointed out, if I cater to one person's whims, it throws off everyone else's schedule. I'm causing trouble for all the other people who have to rearrange their plans."

"I see. I guess that makes sense." Daniel leaned over and whispered in a low bass voice that tickled her senses, "About my *daed*, don't let him fool you. He's terrified that physical therapy will be painful, so he fakes sleep."

Standing only a few inches away, Daniel's lips almost touched Fern's ear. His closeness and the puff of breath swirling past her ear awakened long-buried yearnings. Suppressing a shiver, she stepped sideways to put more distance between them. But she couldn't retreat far enough to dampen his appeal. The minute she'd seen Daniel, watched his kindness toward his *Daed*, she'd been drawn to him. He stirred an ache deep inside for a man's closeness and care. For the warmth of a home and family.

It had been so long. She'd worked hard to tamp down those wishes and care for her *daed* and Lyddie. *I could never go through that pain. Never ever again.*

❄

Daniel wished Fern wasn't so nervous around him. He hadn't meant to crowd her, but her sweetness acted like a magnet, drawing him toward her against his will. She'd been unfailingly kind to *Daed* despite his gripes.

"I'm sorry *Daed* gave you such a hard time," he said.

Fern glanced at him in surprise. "I didn't notice that."

Daniel couldn't believe it. She was probably only being polite because she was talking to the grumbler's son. "So grouchy patients don't bother you?" he teased.

Fern only smiled. "When people are grumpy, they're pining for love. Instead of asking for love, they try to cover up their needs and push people away."

"But I'm here for *Daed* every day. I love him. How do I get him to see that?"

"I suspect your *daed*'s lonely when you're not here. It's hard for him being away from home." Her caring smile made Daniel's heart flip over in his chest. "Your *daed* may believe if you loved him, you'd take him home."

"He begs me to do that every time I come, but he needs to be here for therapy." Even if Daniel had to bear the brunt of *Daed*'s frustration, he'd make sure his father's broken hip healed properly.

Fern patted his arm, sending sparks jolting through him. "You're doing the right thing, but it's hard to take the blame." She checked the large clock on the wall. "I'm sorry, but I need to go."

Daniel wished she could stay longer to chat, but he'd already taken up a lot of her time. "I didn't mean to keep you from your job."

"It's all right. It's been a pleasure talking to you." Fern's cheeks reddened, and she ducked her head. Then she turned and scurried from the room.

Chapter Two

When *Mamm* arrived at school soon after lunch, Lyddie bounced at her desk. She must be here to pick me up early. Good thing the desk legs were nailed down to pine planks to keep them still, or the metal desk legs would have beat a tattoo on the dark wooden floor.

Ever since Lyddie had started at this new one-room schoolhouse, she'd been bashful. Whenever her teacher, Ruthie, asked her questions, Lyddie only hung her head and stared down at her hands clasped on her desk. The answers bubbled up inside, but she couldn't force them past her pressed-together lips. If she opened her mouth, she might burst into tears. And she'd promised *Mamm* she wouldn't cry.

Maybe *Mamm* would take her home now before they went outside for afternoon recess. Then she'd be spared the embarrassment of standing alone while everyone played. The first few days she'd been here, other scholars had invited her to play, but she only stepped back and shook her head. Now they all left her alone.

She pretended not to care, but inside she ached with loneliness. She missed her friends from Charm. They would have understood she sometimes needed to be by herself. But they always offered to include her. If she chose not to play, they still smiled at her and asked the next day in case she'd changed her mind. Once in a while, she said *yes*. But most of the time, she hung back.

Lyddie waited on the edge of her seat for the teacher to dismiss her. She'd jump up and escape from the strange room, her unknown classmates, and her teacher's frown. Her teacher's frown wasn't an *eyebrows-scrunched-together, about-to-yell* frown. It was a *deep-creases-above-the-nose, worried-about-you* frown. The kind of frown that made Lyddie squirm.

She didn't mean to cause trouble or upset her teacher. She just couldn't talk. Not now. Maybe not ever. A big part of it was being shy, but right now all her words tangled together inside—a huge ball of misery.

Even Ruthie's smile when *Mamm* entered held a hint of worry. Instead of dismissing Lyddie, her teacher motioned *Mamm* to a folding chair in the back of the room. Then Ruthie called Lyddie's grade up front to answer questions about the reading they'd finished at their seats.

When Ruthie called on Lyddie, she ducked her head and pinched her lips together. Behind her, Lyddie imagined *Mamm*'s gaze boring into her back, imagined her disappointment at Lyddie's disrespect.

As soon as Ruthie dismissed them, Lyddie shuffled back to her seat, staring at her feet so she wouldn't have to meet *Mamm*'s *you-know-better-than-that* frown. So many frowns directed in her direction from the teacher, the scholars, and even *Mamm*.

After the older students had their math checked, Ruthie tapped the bell on her desk. Like in Lyddie's old school, that was the signal to sit up straight and tall and get ready to go outside for recess.

The scholars put away their books and pencils. A few jumped to their feet, but the rest stood to file out in the orderly manner

Ruthie expected. Lyddie wanted to run to *Mamm*, bury her head in *Mamm*'s apron, and hide. She waited for her turn. Row by row, the little ones first, they went to the cloakroom to get their coats and bonnets. Most boys pulled on stocking caps because it was cold outside. Everyone marched to the door in a straight line.

Her teacher in Ohio never made them do this. Mim would announce recess, and everyone would scramble for the door. Mim only laughed and opened the door so they could tumble out onto the playground.

When Lyddie complained about the differences to *Mamm*, she only said, *Every teacher is different. You need to obey Ruthie's rules.*

Lyddie sighed. The only good things about lining up were that nobody knew you didn't have a partner, you were supposed to face forward so she didn't have to talk to anyone, and it took much longer to get outside. That meant less time alone.

Lyddie wanted to run to *Mamm*, but she didn't know if Ruthie would approve. Her teacher didn't like scholars getting out of line. As Lyddie passed, *Mamm* smiled. Relief flooded through Lyddie, and she beamed. Maybe she wouldn't face an afterschool lecture.

After all the children had exited, Ruthie beckoned to *Mamm*, inviting her out on the playground. Ordinarily, Lyddie hid behind a huge oak tree and shivered in the cold. Today she didn't rush to her usual spot.

A few of the other children glanced in Lyddie's direction, but none of them came over to invite her to play. In one way, it was a relief. She didn't have to figure out what to say, how to make friends.

Wrapping her arms around herself, she pretended not to notice. *I don't care,* she repeated over and over to herself. But that wasn't quite true. Even if she didn't want to play with them, their rejection still hurt.

Lyddie skirted the perimeter of the playground and edged closer to *Mamm* and Ruthie, who had their heads together, talking in low voices, while they studied Lyddie with worried expressions.

❄

Ruthie's comments about Lyddie flowed into Fern's ears, but her heart followed her daughter's progress around the playground. Lyddie scuffed her feet and stared at the ground as if to avoid eye contact with anyone. Her daughter had always been bashful, but since they'd moved to Pennsylvania, she'd crawled so deeply inside herself, Fern wondered if her daughter would ever come out. Right now, Fern wanted to scoop her little daughter into her arms and wrap her in a tight hug.

But she forced herself to tune back into the teacher.

"All of the other parents have made outfits for the Christmas program," Ruthie said. "I'll get you the bolt of fabric from the closet before you go."

"*Danke*." Fern tried to sound grateful while she sighed inwardly. One more project to add to her list. She'd have to sew Lyddie's dress completely by hand. She'd sold her sewing machine, her furniture, and almost everything else they owned so she and Lyddie could afford to move here.

Making matching dresses and boys' shirts for school programs had long been a tradition. No matter how much time it took, she'd sew Lyddie's dress. She didn't want her daughter even more isolated.

"I've been thinking," Ruthie said, "It would be nice to present our Christmas songs and poems at the rehab center. So many from the nearby Amish communities are patients."

"What a lovely idea!" Most of the patients Fern cared for would enjoy hearing the children sing.

"I also had another idea. One I'm hoping you'll help with." Ruthie nudged Fern's elbow and tilted her head in Lyddie's direction.

Lyddie had slipped close enough to hear but had turned her back to them and most of the other children. Her daughter appeared to be gazing at the rows of golden stubble lining the fields beside the schoolhouse. But Lyddie's posture and alertness made it clear she had no interest in the dried cornstalks.

Fern had no problem with Lyddie listening to their conversation. She'd share it with her daughter when they got home.

Ruthie shrugged. "I'm sure Lyddie won't tell anyone until I announce it to the class. If we get permission to do it. That's where you come in."

"Me?" Fern yanked her focus from Lyddie to Ruthie.

"*Jah*, you. You work at the rehab center, so I hoped you'd be willing to talk to them."

"About what?" As a new employee, Fern doubted she'd have any influence on their decisions. Although she was pretty sure if she mentioned the Christmas program idea to the program coordinator at the center, Darla would love it.

"I'd like to take the children to the center once a week. I thought they could each be assigned one patient who'll be there for at least several more weeks. The scholars could interview the residents about their lives and childhood. Then they could write reports."

"That sounds interesting."

Ruthie smiled. "I'm glad you think so. I believe it will help the patients as well as the children."

"*Jah*," Fern agreed. "Many of the residents get lonely during the day. Having company would be good for them."

"Great. Then would you be able to talk to the rehab center to help me set this up?"

Fern hesitated. "I'm new there." She didn't know all of the center staff or who'd be in charge of permission.

Lyddie scooted backward, moving closer to them.

If Fern wanted her daughter to be less timid, maybe she

needed to demonstrate her own bravery. "I can ask around tomorrow to see who has to approve this and let you know."

"*Wunderbar.*" Ruthie beamed. "I hope we can work this out. With the rehab center so close, it will be a short walk for the scholars."

"That's so."

Ruthie called for the scholars to line up, and Lyddie was one of the first in line. Until Ruthie asked one of the boys to hold open the schoolhouse door, the other children chattered, but Lyddie stood silent and ignored.

The minute the scholars entered the room, they quietly hung up their coats and headed to their seats. Ruthie beckoned to Fern and headed into the cloakroom.

"Here's the fabric." Ruthie pulled the last of a bolt of forest green fabric from a shelf overhead. Then she lifted a binder from the ledge above the coat hooks. "This is Lyddie's script for the Christmas program. Several days ago, I suggested she take it home to practice. We only have about two and half weeks. So far, she hasn't recited her poem."

"I'm so sorry." Fern would speak to Lyddie. Her reluctance to be in the program was understandable. But Fern wouldn't allow her daughter to treat her teacher with disrespect.

Ruthie eyes filled with sadness. "I understand she's timid, but we need to find a way to help her talk to others." She tapped a finger on the binder. "I gave her two silent parts and one short speaking part. I debated about adding more, but. . ."

"I understand." Asking Lyddie to do more than one speaking part would tie her daughter up in knots.

"First of all, I worried about asking her to memorize too much so close to the show." Ruthie nibbled on her lower lip for a moment. "And with her not responding in class, I'd rather not put her on the spot more than once."

"*Danke*. And I'll talk to Lyddie about participating in class."

"I'd appreciate that." Ruthie pivoted and headed for the front of the room. "I'm glad you came."

"I am too." Clutching the bolt of fabric and Lyddie's program binder, Fern slipped from the cloakroom.

Her heart went out to her daughter, who sat facing front. Head drooping, Lyddie drew circles on the desktop with her finger as Ruthie spoke to the class. Fern hoped Lyddie was paying attention to the lesson.

After easing the door open so she wouldn't disturb the scholars, Fern stepped outside into the chilly November air. Earlier, she'd been so intent on talking to Ruthie, Fern hadn't noticed the temperature dropping. Now the sun hung lower on the horizon, and she bent her head and hunched her shoulders into her cloak to ward off the cold.

The brisk walk to the rehab center warmed and invigorated her. As she approached the entrance to the parking lot, a buggy came up behind her. Fern moved to the right and hugged the gravel shoulder. She motioned for the buggy to go around her, but after the horse passed, the driver slowed.

"Fern?" Daniel's voice washed over her. "I'd offer you a ride, but you're almost there."

She laughed. "I think I can manage the few hundred feet to the door."

"I'll see you later then." He smiled and turned his horse toward the hitching post.

Fern wanted to linger until he tied up his horse, but she'd already taken enough time from her shift. Martha, one of the other aides, had agreed to cover for her so she could visit Lyddie's school, but now she'd have to do part of Martha's evening shift.

By the time she signed in and got her list of tasks from Martha, Daniel had entered the lobby. He stopped her as she headed down the hall. "Do you live far from here? I could pick you up."

The thought of riding in his buggy heated her face. As much as she'd love to do that, she couldn't accept. Besides, their schedules didn't match. "These aren't my normal hours. Today I took a little time off to visit the schoolhouse up the road. They want to do a program here."

She avoided mentioning Lyddie. She didn't have time for long explanations. She had work to do. And she had no way to express her roiling emotions over her daughter's loneliness.

Fern ducked her head so he couldn't see the eagerness in her eyes. "*Danke* for your kind offer, though." She couldn't resist peeping up at him through her lashes.

If she wasn't mistaken, he appeared disappointed. So was she. Now she'd spend the rest of her shift imagining a buggy ride together.

Chapter Three

Daniel stared after Fern as she headed down the hall. What had made him offer to pick her up? Well, she'd cut him off quickly after that.

Spending his teen years caring for *Mamm* hadn't allowed time for courting. If he'd had those teen years, maybe he'd have learned more about dating from some of his friends. Instead, he was more awkward around women than he would have been at sixteen. Now when he had a chance to talk to the nicest woman he'd ever met, he had no idea how to keep a conversation going.

A blast of chilly air hit Daniel in the back, making him realize he'd been standing there staring off into space. He turned to see a young girl standing in the doorway. When he smiled at her, she forced her lips into a stiff smile, then quickly ducked her head. The gesture reminded him of Fern's shyness earlier, and he wanted to put the girl at ease.

"How are you?" he asked. "Did you just come from school?"

Instead of answering, the girl scuttled around him and went to sit on a chair in the farthest corner of the lobby with her back to everyone. Then she pulled out a book and started reading.

So much for his skills with women. Fern scurried off soon after she saw him, and this young girl acted as if he were invisible.

Daniel sighed and hurried down the hallway to *Daed*'s room, bracing himself for a barrage of negativity. Just once, he wished he could walk into the room to see *Daed* smiling. Even better would be to hear an upbeat report of his day.

"You're late," *Daed* barked when Daniel opened the door.

"Sorry. I was talking to someone."

"I wish it had been me." Although his tone was accusing, it held an underlying note of plaintiveness that touched Daniel. It was difficult for *Daed* to be here alone all day.

"It is now," Daniel pointed out. "What did you want to talk about?"

He sank into the chair near *Daed*'s bed to listen to the usual litany of complaints. Although he put on a sympathetic expression, his mind wandered to Fern. He jolted back to the conversation when *Daed* said her name.

"What?"

"Weren't you listening?" *Daed* demanded. Then without waiting for an answer, he plunged on. "This new aide named Martha came to take me for PT. That's what they call physical therapy around here, you know?"

Daniel hid a smile. As far as he knew, that was a common abbreviation anywhere.

"Anyway, I'd gotten ready to go because Fern takes me, and she's so nice."

His *daed* had said something positive about someone? That stunned Daniel so much, he almost missed the rest of the story.

"If I'd known this Martha was coming, I'd have pretended to sleep. I told her I didn't want her to take me, I wanted Fern. But she informed me she was taking Fern's place because Fern had an appointment."

Daniel wondered if that was the appointment she'd mentioned at the schoolhouse. "I hope you didn't give Martha a hard time."

Rather than answering, *Daed* looked away.

"You did, didn't you?" Daniel pressed him. "*Daed,* I don't understand why you're acting this way. Is this how God would want you to treat the staff?"

"*Neh.*" At least he had the grace to look ashamed.

"Then why do you do it? You were never like this at home."

"*Jah,* I was. I complained about your *mamm*. . ." He swallowed hard. "Not to you, but to God. It just didn't seem fair she had to suffer."

"I know," Daniel said softly. *Mamm* had rheumatoid arthritis that ended up crippling her.

"Every time they put me in the wheelchair, I think of her." *Daed* rubbed his forehead.

Poor *Daed*. Losing *Mamm* had been devastating. Then he'd broken his hip soon after. The surgery had been painful, and he was still struggling to recover. *Daed* had always been so active. Now he was confined to bed for weeks.

Be patient with him, Daniel. He's been through a lot.

Fern tapped at the door. "It's time for supper. Would you like to eat in the dining room?

Daed shook his head.

"Are you sure?" Fern asked. "It might be nice for you to get to know other people."

To Daniel's surprise, *Daed* answered in a civil tone. "Not tonight. I'd rather stay here. I have my son for company."

Fern seemed to be a softening influence on him. Then she turned to Daniel. "Shall I bring you a meal too?"

Lost in her brilliant green eyes, Daniel struggled to put together a coherent thought. She'd asked him a question, but he'd forgotten what it was.

Daed's sharp tone cut through his confusion. "Yes, bring him a meal too." He hesitated a moment, then added, "Please."

Why did *Daed* treat this pretty aide differently from everyone else? But when she smiled at both of them, Daniel understood completely.

❄

Although Fern's attention remained on Daniel even after she broke their gaze, she forced herself to answer Moses. "Two meals coming up." Despite her rapid pulse, she tried to keep her tone casual. "I'll be back as soon as I seat everyone staying in this wing."

Daniel's soft *danke* as she exited the room echoed in her ears while she made her rounds. This wing held patients who used wheelchairs, so Fern traveled from room to room, pushing them into the dining room. Most people appreciated the chance to socialize. Moses was the only one in this hall who refused to participate.

Fern hoped she could convince Moses to get involved in more activities. It might help him emotionally. As she'd mentioned to Daniel, much of his *daed*'s grumpiness probably came from loneliness.

Speaking of that, Fern passed through the lobby and veered toward the chair in the far corner of the room, where her daughter sat curled up with a book. She worried about Lyddie's isolation too. One good thing about Lyddie's bashfulness was that she'd never cause trouble, and most likely, the rehab staff probably wouldn't even notice she was around. Perhaps she should have asked permission, but with the huge padded chairback blocking Lyddie from view and her daughter's quietness, nobody had even questioned what a young girl was doing here every day after school.

"Lyddie?" Fern set a hand on her daughter's head. "Are you all right?"

Raising her gaze from the book, Lyddie smiled and nodded.

Of course she was. She was in a secluded corner by herself with a book. That was Lyddie's preferred setting.

"I have to stay later tonight because someone covered my hours while I went to your school. We won't leave until seven thirty." Usually they left at five.

"That's all right," Lyddie murmured, her attention back on her book.

"I'll bring you some supper after I've taken care of everyone in my hallway."

Lyddie's absentminded *danke* told Fern her daughter had retreated deep into a story.

A short while later, Fern trundled the food cart to Moses's room at the end of the hall. She handed trays to both men. "Enjoy your meals." Although she longed to linger, she had meals to deliver in another wing. "I'll be back later for the trays."

Fern hurried through her deliveries, then carried a tray to Lyddie. As staff, she was entitled to a free meal during working hours, although it often meant nibbling on the go if it wasn't break time or gobbling down the food in fifteen minutes if it was. Her half-hour breaks never seemed to come when the food was hot, so for her, it meant eating a cold meal long after everyone else had finished.

Today she'd missed her meal break altogether because she wanted to get to the schoolhouse sooner. And now, she handed her supper to her daughter. Lyddie's appreciative smile eased some of the grumbling hollowness of Fern's stomach.

And a few minutes later, as she collected trays from Moses and Daniel, her spirit overflowed with happiness. Their smiles and kind words filled the loneliness in her heart.

As she was leaving the room, her stomach gurgled loudly. Embarrassed, Fern hurried through the door to stack the trays on the cart, but Daniel followed her.

"Did you have supper?" he asked.

"Not yet," Fern answered, sliding both trays onto the cart shelves. She wouldn't have a meal until she and Lyddie arrived back at their room later tonight.

"Will you get a break soon?"

Keeping her back to him, Fern squeezed her eyes shut for a moment. The concern in his voice brought up that longing again to be in a relationship with a man who cared about her, treated her tenderly. "I already had my breaks for today."

"But you need to eat something."

"I will," she assured him, "as soon as my shift is over. I'd better go. I have a lot of trays to collect in the other hall." And people to wheel back to their rooms after dinner. Fern pushed the rattling cart down the hall.

❄

Daniel stood in the hallway, wishing he could help. He stuck his head in the doorway. "Be right back, *Daed*. I'm going to get a few snacks."

His *daed*'s bushy eyebrows bunched together. "But you just finished eating." Then light dawned in his eyes. "Ohhh. Good idea, son."

Wow! Had *Daed* said something upbeat again? Fern definitely was a miracle worker.

Humming to himself, Daniel walked down the hall and through the lobby, heading for the small alcove that housed several snack machines. Unsure what Fern would prefer, he selected a pack of cheese and crackers along with a bag of peanuts. Those would be filling and hold off her hunger pangs. Then he picked a bag of chips and a candy bar. Most people liked chocolate. He hoped he'd made good choices.

As he crossed the lobby, he noticed the young girl he'd spoken to earlier practically hidden by the overstuffed chair. She was still absorbed in her book. If she hadn't eaten anything, she must be hungry too.

He wound his way back to the machines and duplicated his earlier purchases and added one package of brightly colored small candies. Then he headed toward the girl, his arms filled with snacks.

"Are you hungry?" he asked as he approached her chair.

She glanced up at him and blinked. Then her gaze drifted down to his full arms, and her eyes widened.

"Would you like some?" Daniel asked.

The girl shook her head. "N-no." Then belatedly she added a barely audible *danke* before ducking her head.

"You must be hungry. It's past suppertime, and you've been here since late afternoon."

No response. Daniel remembered being shy like that when he was in school.

"Tell you what. I'll leave a few of these in case you get hungry." He bent down to set several snacks on the table.

An empty meal tray had been stashed under her chair. "Looks like you might have already eaten," Daniel said as he stood. He tilted his chin in the direction of the tray. "Maybe you'll want a snack later."

Another soft *danke* floated after him as he strode away.

He entered the room and dumped the remaining snacks on *Daed*'s bedside table.

"I hope she likes those," *Daed* said, his tone implying she probably wouldn't.

"If she doesn't," Daniel told him, "you can eat them."

"I guess," *Daed* mumbled.

Surprised that *Daed* hadn't gone on the attack, Daniel settled into the chair to listen to his *daed* recount his horrible experience with Martha—the poor woman's only sin seemed to be that she'd taken Fern's place—and the awful physical therapist.

If Daniel hadn't seen the physical therapy room, he might have believed *Daed* had been chained to instruments of medieval torture. But perhaps to *Daed* they felt like that. Daniel had never endured PT, so he had no idea if *Daed* was telling the truth or exaggerating.

Daniel usually waited until one of the aides came in to prepare *Daed* for bed. Then he slipped out. But tonight he worried about Fern not having something to eat.

When *Daed* stopped for breath, Daniel stood. "Maybe I should take these to Fern." He pointed to the snacks on the table.

"*Jah*, she shouldn't be working without eating."

"I'll be back as soon as I find her." Daniel gathered the packages and headed down the hall.

As he crossed the lobby, he checked the back corner. The small bag of candy had disappeared. Smiling to himself, Daniel wandered up and down the halls in search of Fern

"Not that way," a high-pitched voice snarled. "Can't you do anything right?"

Daniel glanced in the room as he passed to see Fern easing an elderly woman from a wheelchair into bed.

"You're hurting me," the woman whined.

"I'm so sorry, Myrtle." Gingerly, she set the woman on the bed. "Is that better?"

A low grumble was Myrtle's only response.

Fern reached for the bedcovers. "I'll just tuck you in."

"You forgot my bed socks," Myrtle snapped.

"So I did." Fern headed to the small dresser across the room. "Will these do?" She held up a pair of green fuzzy socks.

"No. I want pink," Myrtle insisted.

"Of course." Fern pulled out pink ones. As she headed back to Myrtle's bed, she glanced toward the doorway.

Her eyes widened, so she'd seen him. But she turned her full attention to her patient. After she pulled on Myrtle's pink socks, she followed all the bossy directions and criticisms until all the sheets, blankets, and pillows had been arranged and rearranged multiple times.

"Shall I leave the light on or turn it off?"

"Turn it off. It's bedtime."

Daniel eased the door shut to cut down the light from the hallway, and Fern shot him a grateful glance before it closed.

The switch flipped, and Fern cracked the door open.

"You're not going to leave me here alone in the dark. I can't see anything."

The old woman's plaintive voice tugged at Daniel's heartstrings.

"Shall I turn on the nightlight in the bathroom?" Fern asked.

Daniel held the door slightly open so she'd have a little light to see and was rewarded with a brilliant smile when she returned.

"*Danke*," she said after she'd slipped into the hallway and closed the door behind her. "That was thoughtful of you."

Dazzled by her smile, Daniel forgot why he'd come.

Fern gestured to the pile of snacks in his hands. "I guess supper didn't fill you up."

"What? Oh, these? They're, um, for you."

"Me?"

"You said you hadn't had supper, so I thought maybe. . ."

She just stared at him.

"If you don't like any of these, I can get something else."

"No, it's not that. It's just"—she blinked several times—"you didn't have to do that."

Daniel could have sworn her eyes had moisture in them, unless the florescent lights overhead were making them sparkle. He'd only brought her a few simple snacks. What had caused that reaction?

He held out the crackers and the peanuts. "I thought these might be the most filling."

"*Danke*," she said in a choked voice.

He followed her as she moved down the hall to the next room. The paper crackled when she opened the crackers, and she ate two hurriedly.

Daniel gave her a sympathetic glance. "I thought my *daed* was a trial for you, but I didn't realize you had to deal with that from other patients too." It didn't seem fair when she went out of her way to be kind.

"Most people are a joy. They're grateful for our assistance and usually very appreciative."

"I'm glad to hear that. I'd hate to think of you having to deal with nastiness every day." He wished he could protect her.

"Myrtle's usually pretty sweet, but tonight's she's tired and in pain. We have to make allowances for that." Fern slipped the crackers into her dress pocket. "I appreciate these."

She tapped at the door. "Eli, it's Fern."

"Come in, come in," Eli boomed. "I've been waiting for you."

Daniel couldn't help being a little jealous of the attention Fern lavished on the good-looking Amish man confined to his bed. When he reached for her hand and held it longer than he should, Daniel paced down the hall. He had no right to be upset.

He should be back with *Daed,* but he wanted to give Fern more of the snacks. And if he were honest, he wanted her to smile at him the way she'd just smiled at Eli.

Chapter Four

When Fern exited Eli's room, Daniel stood outside, waiting for her. At her surprised expression, his face reddened.

"I wanted to be sure you had a few more snacks," he said. "You really should eat so you don't pass out. You'll be no good to the patients if you do."

"True." Fern smiled at his teasing. She'd gone without meals many times, but she didn't want to hurt his feelings. She accepted the peanuts and candy bar. Those she could slip into her other pocket. "*Danke* for these. I'm afraid the chips would end up as crumbs in my pocket. Perhaps your *daed* would like them for a bedtime snack."

"I'm sure he would. I hope you'll eat the other things. I wouldn't like to think of you fainting."

At his tender words, her pulse sped even faster than it normally did around him. "Don't worry. I won't." She took two more crackers from her pocket. "I'll eat these now." As much as she'd like to stand here talking to him outside each door, she had work to do. "I'm sorry," she said, "but I need to get back to work."

"I apologize for holding you up."

"I think we've had this conversation before." Her cheeks

flamed when she realized what she'd said the last time. She hoped he didn't remember. Ducking her head, she scurried toward the next room.

Before she entered, she turned to watch him walk down the hall. Still chewing the crackers, she tapped at the door. When Bertha called out for her to come in, Fern swallowed quickly. She needed to keep her thoughts on her work, but her mind stayed filled with Daniel.

She'd never been so grateful to sign out. Today had been an especially long and trying day. The snacks Daniel had brought her had been a lifesaver. Only she'd made a fool of herself by tearing up. She had no way to explain how much his simple act of kindness meant to her.

She'd been carrying heavy burdens for so long, and her whole life had revolved around caring for others. To have someone think about her and be concerned about her welfare touched her deeply.

Lyddie still sat in the corner chair where she'd left her. The tray from supper lay under her seat. Fern sighed. She'd forgotten to pick up the tray. Now she'd need to run down to the kitchen and rinse everything on it.

"*Mamm*?" Lyddie glanced up in relief. "Are you done now?"

"Almost. I'll have to wash your dishes."

On the coffee table in front of Lyddie, wrappers and unopened snack packages fanned out in a semicircle.

"Where did you get those?"

Lyddie shrugged. "Some man gave them to me. He thought I'd missed dinner, and he didn't want me to be hungry."

Odd that the snacks were the exact same ones Daniel had chosen for her. "What did he look like?"

Her daughter's description matched Daniel, right down to his light green shirt. The sparkly green eyes clinched it. "Did he ask you any questions? Does he know you're my daughter?"

"No, I didn't talk to him. He just walked up to me, his hands filled with snacks and gave me half."

It seemed Daniel made a habit of feeding the hungry. Fern laughed to herself. He certainly was following the Bible's command, although she was pretty sure Jesus hadn't meant people like her and Lyddie. For all she knew, though, Daniel also handed out meals to the homeless.

Or maybe he viewed her and Lyddie as poor and needy. Their dresses were worn, their shoes old and scuffed. Fern shook her head. She had to set him straight. She and Lyddie might be struggling right now, but they weren't charity cases.

❄

"What took you so long?" *Daed* groused as soon as Daniel walked through the door.

"It took a while for me to find her," Daniel explained. "And once I did, she was so busy, I had to follow her down the hall between patients before I could give her the snacks."

Daed's loud harrumph showed he wasn't fooled by Daniel's story. "I'm sure that was a trial."

Daniel ignored *Daed*'s waggling eyebrows and insinuating tone. Instead, he pretended the comment had been neutral. "Actually, it wasn't a hardship at all. Watching her work was interesting."

"And it was only her work that interested you?"

No, it had been much more. Her personality, her eyes, her smile—all entranced him.

But he wasn't about to tell *Daed* that. In fact, it might be time to turn the conversation to his father's behavior. "You know what bothered me the most?" Daniel asked, but he didn't pause long enough for *Daed* to answer the question. "I couldn't believe people were mean to her. She was trying to help them, take care of them. Did they appreciate it? No, they did not. They snapped at her, criticized her—"

"That's not fair," *Daed* interrupted. "She's the kindest worker here."

"I agree. Although all the workers I've met are very nice. I wouldn't say any of them deserve to be mistreated."

Daed's indignation over Fern's treatment faded, and the fire burning in his eyes died. He hung his head. "I suppose you're referring to me."

Daniel longed to say, *If the hat fits, wear it,* but he kept silent. It wasn't his place to criticize his *daed*. And it seemed God was convicting him.

"I'll try to do better," *Daed* said, "but it's difficult. Especially when I'm stuck in here. And I'm lonely and in pain." He pressed his lips together. "I suppose that's no excuse."

Daniel hoped Martha would get an apology tomorrow, along with everyone else whose feelings *Daed* had hurt.

❄

The next morning, Fern discussed Ruthie's idea with her supervisor and the center's program coordinator.

"I love it," Darla said. "I wish they had enough students to meet with everyone in the center. So many of these people are lonely. I'm sure a chance to talk about themselves and see a cute young child would brighten anyone's day."

"I'm glad you like the idea. Is there anything you need me to do?" Fern asked.

"A list with the kids' names and ages would be good. And maybe a few details about them like hobbies, interests, personalities. Then I'll match each of them with a good partner."

"That's a great idea." Fern couldn't wait to tell Ruthie about the center's approval.

She was so excited about it, she decided to stop by the schoolhouse on her lunch break. Before she told Ruthie, Fern sought out

Lyddie first. Her daughter's eyes widened, evidently surprised to see her *mamm* at her school again.

Fern stood quietly in the back of the room while Ruthie finished the small group lesson she was teaching. As the battery-powered clock ticked away at the front of the room, Fern fidgeted. She had to be back in twenty minutes. Finally, Ruthie sent the children back to their seats with an assignment and walked to the back of the room.

"The rehab center would love to have the children," Fern told her. "In fact, Darla, the program coordinator, mentioned she wished the children could visit all the patients."

"We should take advantage of that," Ruthie said. "For the next two weeks, I think one person for each child will be enough. But maybe we could plan to do more visits when the weather gets warmer in the spring."

"I need to go soon, but they'd like a list of the students." One eye on the clock, Fern rushed through Darla's suggestions.

Ruthie's eyes lit up. "What a wonderful idea! We'll work on the list this afternoon, and I'll send it with Lyddie. She'll be walking to the rehab center after school, right?"

"*Jah*. That would be great. Darla said you could come next week, so maybe you can also include the days and times that would be best."

"I'll do that," Ruthie said.

"Good." Fern flashed her daughter a special smile before she exited. The disappointment on Lyddie's face made Fern ache inside. Had Lyddie been hoping to leave school early? She should have taken time to explain to her daughter.

Fern ran all the way back to the center and arrived out of breath and panting. She stood in the lobby for a few minutes to get her breathing under control. Then she hung up her cloak and bonnet, smoothed down her apron, and started her afternoon rounds.

She hoped Ruthie could transfer her excitement to the

students, including Lyddie. Fern had a feeling Lyddie would dread the visits. If only they could find a way to encourage Lyddie to participate in school activities. Maybe if Fern explained her daughter's shyness, Darla would find a good match for Lyddie. Someone quiet, someone who liked books, someone who'd be patient with Lyddie's bashfulness.

When Lyddie arrived in the late afternoon with her teacher's list, Fern skimmed it, searching for her daughter's name. Although all the other students had several descriptive phrases after their names, Ruthie had written after Lyddie's only one: *extremely shy*.

"What would you like me to put after your name?" Fern asked Lyddie.

Her daughter shrugged. "Do I have to do this?"

Fern nodded. "I expect you to do everything your teacher asks of you." That reminded her. Yesterday she'd stored the fabric and Lyddie's program binder in her employee locker downstairs. As soon as she went on break, she'd give Lyddie the binder.

"Can I read now?" Lyddie asked.

Fern nodded, and her daughter rushed over to her usual corner chair. With a sigh, Fern made a detour by Darla's office to drop off the list. Just before she knocked, she made a quick notation beside Lyddie's name: *likes to read*.

After Fern handed over the list, Darla held up one of her own. "I went through the records to select thirty people who'll be here until Christmas. That way all the children can stay with the same friend."

"There are only twenty-six students," Fern pointed out.

"I know," Darla said. "I figure we might need a few backups in case anyone says *no*. So far, no one has." She ran a finger over a series of green checkmarks beside the names. "That's how many have agreed to be a friend."

More than a dozen names had been checked off. "That's *wunderbar*."

"It is, isn't it? The nice thing about selecting the long-term patients is they can attend the Christmas program. Seeing one of their young friends up front will make the night extra special."

"How nice." That was a good idea. Big and small special friends would enjoy each other's company. With the possible exception of her daughter. "I have one special request," Fern said.

Pointing to her daughter's name, she said, "Lyddie is painfully shy, and she struggles to talk to people."

"What about Mary Hess? She used to write columns for the local newspaper."

"That might work," Fern said. Mary Hess was sweet-natured, but very quiet. "Maybe if I tell Lyddie she's a writer, that will make her curious and interested."

"I'll also ask Mary to start the conversation. I'm sure she's done some interesting research she can share."

"That would be really helpful." If Mary started the conversation, Lyddie might respond. She'd at least listen. That might be the best they could hope for.

❄

With Christmas coming, the woodworking business was busier than ever, so Daniel arrived at the rehab center later than usual.

"Where have you been?" *Daed* demanded. "I've been worried sick. What if something had happened to you? How would I know?"

"I had to work late, but I could get a cell phone so I could call the center whenever that happens."

"Daniel Graber," *Daed* thundered, "I can't believe you'd even think such a thing, let alone say it."

So much for *Daed*'s change of heart last night. Daniel hoped he hadn't gone after the staff today. He held up a hand to interrupt *Daed*'s lecture about staying separate from the modern world.

"I was only joking." Although many of his friends secreted cell phones in their pockets, he'd never desired one.

Daed crossed his arms. "That's not something to joke about."

Fern tapped at the door. "Are you ready for physical therapy?" She smiled at *Daed,* but then extended it to Daniel. "Hello. How are you?"

His heartbeat accelerated. Was it his imagination or did she look even prettier than usual today? Or maybe her smile had increased in brilliance. Daniel stared at her wordlessly until his brain kicked in. "F-fine," he managed to stutter.

"Are you coming with us to PT today?" Fern asked.

Of course he was. Anything to spend more time with her. "I wouldn't miss it," he blurted out.

Daed gave him a funny look, and Daniel's face burned. He'd made it sound like watching his *daed* suffer through PT would be *wunderbar*. To cover his embarrassment, Daniel frowned at *Daed.* "Did you miss your appointment again this morning?"

"*Neh,*" Fern answered. "His physical therapist had an appointment this morning, so she came in late."

Daniel pinned *Daed* with a stern look. "I'm sure you still found time to apologize to Martha this morning, though?"

With a sheepish look, *Daed* stared at his knobby hands clenched on the sheet. "Not yet."

"Martha wasn't in here today?"

"Well, she was," *Daed* admitted. "I'll do it tomorrow."

Fern looked from one to the other. Daniel didn't feel it was his place to discuss *Daed*'s behavior. His father could decide if he wanted to confess his faults.

When neither of them explained their conversation, Fern headed to the bed. "Ready, Moses?"

He winced. "What would you do if I said I'm not ready?"

"I'd wait a little while until you were, but if I thought you were only stalling, I'd help you into the wheelchair like this." Fern maneuvered him from the bed to the chair.

Daniel marveled at how such a petite woman could handle *Daed*'s weight. Then she once again gave him that sweet smile that charmed them both. Still in a daze, he followed her out of the room.

❄

With Daniel walking so near her, Fern struggled to catch her breath and to start a conversation. She seized on the first thought that came to mind.

"The schoolhouse down the road is bringing scholars here next week to pair up with patients. Would you like that, Moses?"

He turned to look at her, his face twisted in a scowl. "They want us to babysit? That's the teacher's job."

"Oh, no, not babysit. The children would be coming to spend time with you and learn about your lives. They'll use their experiences to write an essay."

"I'd scare them off," Moses muttered.

"You could try being nice," Daniel suggested, then turned to Fern. "It sounds like a great idea." His encouraging smile took some of the sting from his father's reaction.

Fern stared into his eyes so long, her pace slowed.

"Why are we stopping in the middle of the hallway?" Moses's demand brought her back to reality with a thud.

Fern averted her eyes and pushed the wheelchair faster to make up for lost time. And although Daniel's clean-shaven face indicated he was single, she had no business pining over him. She had a job and a daughter who needed her time and attention. She only wished she could get her heart rate and breathing under control.

When they reached the PT room, Fern turned Moses over to Debbie and prepared to leave, but Daniel stopped her.

"Was that why you were at the schoolhouse yesterday?" The

admiration in his eyes made her uncomfortable. "You always think about other people's needs, don't you?"

Fern lowered her head and stared at the floor. "Not always." In fact, if he could peek into her head right now, he'd find it filled with her own needs and longings.

"Despite my *daed*'s reaction, I think talking with a scholar would be good for him. I'm pretty sure he wouldn't bark at a child."

Fern met Daniel's eyes and smiled. "Your *daed*'s never barked at me."

"You're different."

"Not worth barking at?" she said in a teasing tone.

But he stared at her thoughtfully, seriously. Then he shook his head. "It's just that"—his Adam's apple bobbed up and down —"you're special."

No! As much as Fern had wished he'd show an interest in her, now that he had—at least, she thought he had—she wanted to flee. Loving someone only brought heartache.

"I need to get back to work." Fern whirled around. "I forgot to thank you for the snacks last night," she said over her shoulder. "I appreciated them." She stopped before she added that she appreciated him too.

She practically race-walked to the elevator. But putting distance between them wouldn't stop her runaway emotions or runaway heart.

Chapter Five

Daniel hadn't intended to scare her off. This whole dating thing was a puzzle. He was wise enough to know he'd made her uncomfortable. That gave him a clue that when he was around her, he needed to mask his feelings. But if he hid his emotions, how would they connect on a deeper level?

He wished he could discuss it with *Daed*. But talking about it would mean facing ridicule and possible humiliation. And most likely, at some point, *Daed* would bring it up in front of Fern, embarrassing both of them.

Daniel pushed it from his mind as best he could and went over to keep *Daed* company. He forced himself to listen closely to Debbie's directions. At some point he'd have to help with exercises at home, so he asked questions and mentally took notes.

Daed's groan drew Daniel's attention. He'd been so busy concentrating on Debbie's explanations about how hip bones healed, he hadn't glanced at his father.

His *daed's* face glowed bright red, and rivulets of sweat streamed down his forehead. His lips were pressed into a thin, tight line, and his eyes were squeezed shut. A grunting sound came from deep in his chest.

"Is he all right?" Daniel couldn't keep the alarm from his voice.

A loud breath exploded from *Daed*'s mouth. He turned pleading eyes to Debbie. "Can…I…stop?"

She smiled and said in a cheerful voice, "Only two more, Moses. You can do it." Then she turned to Daniel. "It's difficult, but your father's a strong man. All the work he did in the fields gave him well-developed muscles. We can't let them atrophy."

Daniel wasn't sure what atrophy meant, but it didn't sound good. "What would happen then?"

"If he loses that muscle tone, he'll have a hard time regaining it at his age. He's what?"

"Eighty-one," Daniel said.

Debbie's eyebrows shot up. "And you're what? In your thirties?"

Daniel nodded. "Thirty-four." His parents had him very late in life. *Mamm* had been over forty, and *Daed* close to fifty.

Daed finished repeating the exercise, and Debbie cheered.

"Great job, Moses. Only one more. Try taking a deep breath first," she said. "Shallow breathing deprives you of oxygen."

Without even dropping the thread of their conversation, Debbie studied Daniel for a moment. "No beard," she said. "So you've never been married, right?"

"Right." Although Debbie was an *Englischer*, she seemed to know about the Amish. He supposed if she worked with them here at the rehab center, she'd learned a lot.

"Forgive me if this is too personal, but don't most of you Amish get married younger than that?"

"Most do," Daniel mumbled.

"What about you?"

Daniel didn't like the idea of answering questions like this, so he was relieved when Debbie focused on *Daed*.

"That's it, Moses. Now hold for the count of four." She tapped on the metal bar near her hand. "One. Two. Three. Four. Now down. Gently, gently."

Daed slumped back, his eyes closed.

"You can take a few minutes to relax, Moses. Then we have one more machine to go."

As if she hadn't been talking to *Daed* about exercise, she said to Daniel, "You didn't answer my question."

He shrugged. "Haven't found the right one yet, I guess."

"He's. . .pretty. . .slow," *Daed* wheezed out between gasps. "And. . .shy."

Nothing like having your father broadcast your faults to everyone in the room. Daniel shoved his hands in his pockets. At least Fern wasn't here.

Although what *Daed* said had some truth to it, Daniel had another reason. "I needed to take care of *Mamm*," he said quietly. "Rheumatoid arthritis crippled her."

"I'm sorry." Debbie's round face creased into sad lines. "It's a tough disease for some people. Others manage it well."

Debbie gave *Daed* a clean towel and helped him into the wheelchair. "How's she doing?"

Shooting a quick glance at *Daed*, Daniel lowered his voice. "She died six months ago." Losing *Mamm* had left a gaping hole in their lives, and the pain still stayed raw. But as hard as it had been for Daniel, *Daed* had been devastated.

"I'm so sorry." Debbie pushed the wheelchair across the room.

"If *Daed* seems snappish or mean," Daniel whispered, "I hope you'll forgive him."

"I'm used to it," Debbie said as she parked the wheelchair. "It's part of the job."

Fern had said something similar. How did they manage to keep their feelings hidden? Perhaps he could use some lessons.

❄

Fern hoped she hadn't hurt Daniel's feelings by rushing off. She'd been desperate to get away.

Her afternoon schedule kept her busy and harried. Definitely a blessing, because she didn't want to think about Daniel. Yet his eyes haunted her in every corridor, in every room, in every mirror. Wherever she turned he was there.

By suppertime, she'd convinced herself she couldn't face him. How could she ever look him in the eye?

Martha scurried past with a loaded cart. Fern chased after her.

"Is something wrong?" Martha's face took on a look of concern.

Out of breath, both from running and from nervousness, Fern struggled to compose herself. "Could you…do me a…favor?"

"Of course, if I can. What is it?"

Taking in a large gulp of air before making her request, Fern prayed Martha would agree. "If I get the dinner trays, could you take two to the last room in that hallway?" She gestured toward Moses's room. "Thirty-one."

Martha's eyes narrowed. "Is that who I think it is?"

"It's Moses Graber."

Martha winced. "Thought so. Let me think about it while I deliver these meals."

"I'll take my patients to the dining room. Then check back with you." Fern tried not to let her desperation show. "I'll take trays to your last few patients. Six or eight of them? Would that help?"

"You really are desperate, aren't you, honey?" the older woman said. "Not that I blame you. That man has a temper."

"That isn't why—" Fern clamped her mouth shut before she blurted out the real reason. "Tell you what. I'll take care of it all. Even going down to the kitchen for the trays. Okay?"

Martha hesitated. "Well…"

Fern sent her a pleading look, and Martha relented. "I was only teasing, but you'll owe me for this."

"Oh, thank you so much." Fern could have hugged her. "And if you ever need me to do something for you, just let me know."

Martha laughed. "Going into the room with Moses, I feel kind of like Daniel entering the lion's den." She stared at Fern in alarm. "What's the matter? You've gone all pale. You're not going to faint, are you?"

"No, no." At the mention of the name *Daniel,* all the blood drained from Fern's face, leaving her dizzy and lightheaded. Why, out of all the stories in the Bible, had Martha chosen that one? "I'd better go, so I'm not late."

Fern hurried to get everyone into the dining room and then went downstairs to get two trays. She met Martha in the hallway. "I'll take these to the last two rooms, so you'll have two left for room thirty-one." When she came out, she helped Martha deliver the last few trays.

"Thank you," Martha said, then she made a face. "Guess it's time to beard the lion in his den."

"I'm sorry. I shouldn't make you do this."

Martha laughed. "I'm just fooling. We can't let unkind patients get to us. You're new, so I understand you might not have thick enough skin to take the irritation and criticism. But you'll learn."

Fern didn't contradict her. She could ignore the insults, but she couldn't brush off her reaction to Daniel.

❄

When an aide showed up with their dinners, Daniel's anticipation of seeing Fern again

shriveled and died. Was she avoiding him, or had she been scheduled elsewhere tonight?

"Where's Fern?" *Daed* barked. "Why isn't she serving us dinner?"

"Well. . ." The gray-haired, motherly-looking woman fidgeted and looked uncomfortable.

Daniel moved so he blocked *Daed*'s view of the door. He

wouldn't let his father bully her. "I'm sure she's attending to other duties," he said to the woman. "Isn't that right?"

"Martha," *Daed* bellowed, "I want Fern."

"I'm sorry." Martha peered around Daniel to look his father in the eye. "She has other duties." Then she extended the trays. "Where would you like me to put these?"

"I'll take them." Daniel stepped closer so he could take the melamine trays. So this was Martha. The Martha *Daed* was supposed to apologize too.

Before Daniel could say anything, Martha gave him a quick smile and rushed out the door.

Her hurrying away reminded him of Fern, and his spirits sank. Was he destined to chase everyone off?

That gloomy thought kept him occupied throughout dinner. He barely heard *Daed*'s complaints. Maybe he should apologize to Fern.

He wondered if she'd eaten dinner tonight. Maybe he could offer her a snack again. That would at least give him a reason to talk to her. Once they got started, he'd try to find a way to make things right.

He set his tray aside and stretched. "I'm going to get a candy bar. Would you like one?"

"After all this food? We had chocolate pudding for dessert."

Daniel hadn't noticed. He'd been too preoccupied.

"I'm guessing this is less about your sweet tooth and more about you being sweet on someone. Am I right?"

With a shrug, Daniel headed for the door. He stepped into the hallway and turned. "Did you want something?"

"Maybe a pack of those chips you brought me last night."

"Anything else?"

"Nope. That should do it. Oh, and don't take as much time as you did last night."

Daniel couldn't promise that. If he found Fern, he hoped they could have a long talk.

❄

After Fern had finished her usual evening chores, her supervisor asked her to sweep the dining room and Martha's hallway, so they could be mopped.

Fern headed over to tell Lyddie she'd be a bit longer. Her daughter shrugged and went back to the book she was reading. Fern finished the sweeping and was about to return the broom when Daniel stepped from the doorway at the other end of the hall.

He hadn't noticed her because he'd stopped to say something to his *daed*. Fern ducked behind one of the pillars at the lobby entrance and scooted over to where Lyddie sat.

"Could you put this broom away for me? The broom closet's the last door at the end of the hall. The door's partway open."

Lyddie looked at her as if she were crazy. "What?"

Fern didn't have time to repeat the instructions. She thrust the broom into Lyddie's hands. "Broom closet. Very last door." She pointed to Martha's hall.

Then she pushed open the door to the stairs and headed down to her locker. She donned her cloak and bonnet, and picked up her purse. She couldn't believe her cowardice. Asking Martha and then Lyddie to take her place.

But she couldn't face Daniel. At least not yet. Not until she composed herself.

Maybe she'd been mistaken about his comments earlier. She might have read more into them than he'd intended. If so, that was an even greater reason for avoiding him. With the way she'd run off, he probably guessed she'd misinterpreted.

Either way, she'd like to avoid him for a while. She had this weekend off, so if she could leave tonight without seeing him, she'd have the weekend away. Perhaps by Monday, he'd have forgotten.

But she wouldn't forget. She'd have two full days to replay

every detail and make herself more embarrassed. If only she hadn't run. She should have done what she did with her clients. Act casual. Let everything roll off her. Pretend the remarks and looks had no special meaning. Maybe they hadn't.

Instead, her attraction to him had gotten in the way. And after wishing for a man to care about her, as soon as she suspected one might be interested, she'd panicked.

What did you do when your two greatest desires collided? How could she find a warm, close relationship with anyone if she was too scared to love again?

❄

When Daniel reached the snack machines, he bought chips and a candy bar. Last night Fern had eaten the crackers. He dropped in coins and pulled the lever. After picking up that packet, he turned and almost bumped into the young girl from last night.

"Hi," he said. "Would you like some candy again?"

Her eyes wide, she resembled a nervous colt as she shook her head.

"You're here again. Are you visiting someone?" he asked.

Another head shake.

He wondered what it would take to get her to talk. "What's your name?" he asked gently.

She lowered her head and mumbled, "Lyddie."

"So, Lyddie, if you're not visiting anyone, what are you doing here?"

She hesitated so long, he thought she wasn't going to answer. Scuffing her foot on the tile, she said so quietly he had to strain to hear her, "*Mamm* works here."

"I see," Daniel said. "You wait here until she's done?"

With a quick nod, she dashed over to the chair where he'd found her last night and picked up her book.

Not again. Another female had run away from him.

He was even more disappointed after he roamed the halls and didn't find Fern. Maybe it was better he hadn't. Not if all three females he'd tried to talk to today had fled.

❄

On Wednesday afternoon when Ruthie announced the class would be going to the rehab center, Lyddie's stomach scrunched into tight knots. While the other students gathered their pencils and notebooks, Lyddie wrapped her arms around herself, wishing she could disappear.

The other rows were dismissed, one by one, and her enthusiastic classmates put on coats and hats, then hurried to line up by the door.

The closer her turn came, the blob in her stomach grew tighter and heavier. By the time Ruthie nodded for Lyddie's row to go to the cloakroom, she was too sick to move.

"Time to go, Lyddie," Ruthie said, passing Lyddie's desk. "Coat and bonnet on now." Her tone left no room for disobeying.

But after Lyddie stood, Ruthie set a gentle hand on her shoulder. "I know this isn't easy for you, but I think you'll like your partner."

Lyddie doubted that. She'd be too scared to talk to anyone. Sitting in a room for an hour without speaking would be pure torture. Dragging her feet, Lyddie dawdled until she was the last one in line.

Ruthie clapped her hands to calm the bedlam at the door. "I want everyone to have their safety vests on."

On their way to school, the children who walked or used scooters wore fluorescent yellow vests with reflective tape to make them more visible to cars. For today's walk along the country road, they all needed to be seen.

The teacher moved one of the older girls to the front. "You'll be the line leader, Mary. Lyddie, you can bring up the rear."

Lyddie secretly hoped she could slip off once they started walking, but Ruthie stepped into place behind Lyddie.

"This way I can see any stragglers," Ruthie said.

With the teacher on her heels, Lyddie was trapped. She'd have no chance to escape. Each step closer they got, the larger the rock in Lyddie's stomach grew. By the time they entered the lobby, the stone had become a boulder.

Mamm was in the lobby to greet them. "Welcome, everyone. I want to introduce you to the program coordinator here at the rehab center, Darla Zimmerman. I hope you'll all listen carefully as she explains what we're going to do."

Darla motioned for the children to form a semi-circle in front of her. "We're so happy to have you here with us today. Lyddie's mom worked all this out." Darla's eyes crinkled with laugh lines as she singled Lyddie out for a special smile.

Lyddie smiled back, then stared down at the patterns on the floor. Everyone turned to stare, and her cheeks burned.

Mamm moved around the circle and put a hand on Lyddie's shoulder. "I have to get back to work, but don't worry. You'll be fine," she whispered.

"To make this easier for the first day," Darla said, "we've closed the doors to the rooms where your partners are. Each door has one of your names on it." Darla gestured toward the nearest door where a neat construction paper sign had been taped low on the door. "The name underneath yours will be your friend's name."

Lyddie studied the sign Darla had indicated. At the top it said, "Mary Elizabeth." Printed underneath were the words, "Anna Byler."

Her own name would be printed on one of those papers. She'd have to talk to a stranger. Lyddie's stomach zoomed down, down, down. Could your stomach fall so far it landed on the floor? Because hers seemed like it might. Before she could swallow back her fears, Darla added more instructions.

"Tap gently at the door, and wait for your friend to say, 'Come in.' We've set a folding chair near each bed. That way you can sit close. Once you've found your room, please prop open the door."

When Darla waved her hand toward the hallway, everyone scattered looking for the names. "Have fun," she called after them.

Lyddie trudged in the same direction as the others, moving as slowly as she could. How could she ever talk to some stranger? One by one, the other children knocked on doors. Lyddie's name was on a door far down the hall. Most of her classmates had already disappeared into rooms.

Standing in front of the door, Lyddie took a deep breath. She couldn't do this. With a quick glance over her shoulder to be sure nobody was watching, Lyddie snatched the sign from the door and crumpled it into a ball. She kept scrunching.

She couldn't go into this room. All she wanted to do was run away and hide. Could she sneak back up the hall without being seen? Maybe she could sit in her favorite chair until everyone finished and then slip back into the group when they were leaving.

She was at the next-to-the-last door in this hall. It was a long, long way back to the lobby, and she'd have to pass all those open doors.

The other night she'd put away the broom for *Mamm*. The broom closet was at the end of the other hall. This hall had one more door. It was slightly ajar, so it probably was the broom closet. She could hide in there.

Lyddie glanced down the hallway to be sure no one would see her. *Ach*, Darla was headed this way.

The program coordinator stopped to help a first grader prop the door open. Then she took the little girl by the hand and led her into the room.

Panicked, Lyddie ducked into the next doorway and cowered behind the door in the dark. Her heart pounding, she tried to quiet her breathing so she'd hear Darla's squeaky nurse shoes coming down the hallway. If Darla or Ruthie didn't catch her, she'd be safe.

Chapter Six

Lyddie crouched down, trying to make herself smaller and less noticeable in case Darla peeked into the broom closet. It was almost pitch black in here. Nobody could see her. Unless they flicked on the light. Lyddie squeezed her eyes shut and held her breath, tense and alert for footsteps.

"What are you doing?" a voice boomed behind her.

Lyddie jumped. She'd been so worried about Darla, she hadn't glanced around. No mops and brooms surrounded her. Instead, blackout shades had been drawn over the windows, leaving the room in deep shadows. Now that her eyes had adjusted to the darkness, she realized she wasn't in a broom closet but in someone's room.

And that someone was glaring at her.

A bald man with a long white beard. Too frightened to move, Lyddie stared at him, her eyes wide, her heart thumping like a cornered rabbit.

"Did you hear me?" the man demanded. "Why are you in my room?"

His voice was so deep and stern, Lyddie shivered. She was

afraid to answer, but she was even more scared to stay silent. What would he do if she ignored his question?

Lyddie wedged herself deeper into the space behind the door to get farther away from him. Gulping hard, she managed one word, "H-hiding."

"My room is not to be used for hide-and-seek," he snapped. "I'm trying to nap."

"I-I'm n-not p-playing." She had to get out of here, but with Darla in the hallway, Lyddie had no way to escape.

"Close my door. It's letting in light."

Lyddie obeyed.

"I meant to close it when you left."

He sounded so exasperated, Lyddie worried he'd leap out of bed and throw her into the hallway. Right in Darla's path.

"Go on. Get out of here. Leave me alone."

"I-I can't."

"Can't what?"

"Leave."

"Of course you can. Turn the knob and go."

"P-please c-can I stay?" Just for a few minutes until the hall was clear. "I-I'll be quiet."

The elderly man pushed himself up on one elbow. "Come over here," he croaked.

Trembling at his sharp command, Lyddie did what he asked.

"Guess I'm not going to get my nap," he mumbled. Sighing loudly, he struggled to a sitting position. "Lift the shade so I can see you. The cord's right there." He pointed to a thick dangling string with a plastic bell on the end.

Lyddie yanked hard, and the cord flew out of her hand. The shade whipped up to the top with a loud snap, making them both jump.

He blew out a loud breath. "You're supposed to tug it gently. Someone'll have to fix that. I hope you didn't break it."

Lyddie hung her head. "I'm sorry."

"Speak up," he snapped. "I can barely hear you."

"I'm sorry," Lyddie repeated, a little louder, without looking up.

"You should look at people when you speak."

Mamm often told Lyddie that, but looking people in the eye was hard. And scary.

Lyddie forced herself to look up, up, up into the squinting brown eyes under pinched-together eyebrows. She focused on his eyebrows because they looked like fuzzy white caterpillars. And because she didn't like people looking into her eyes.

She shrank back, and the eyebrows lifted high on his forehead. "I'm not going to hurt you," he said in a gruff voice.

Lyddie wasn't sure she believed him. But he hadn't gotten out of bed, and *Mamm* had to push most people in wheelchairs, so maybe she'd be safe if she stayed out of arm's reach.

He winced as he tried to roll over to see her better.

"A-are you hurt?" she asked. If he was, she could outrun him.

"Why else would I be in here?"

His sharp words made her cringe. Did she need to answer him? He'd asked it the way grownups sometimes did when they didn't want an answer. They just wanted you to see you'd said something wrong. Or when they wanted you to apologize.

"I-I'm sorry."

"Stop with the *I'm sorrys*. What's wrong with you?"

Another question she wasn't sure she was supposed to answer. "I-I don't know."

The long, loud sigh he blew out made the hairs on his beard dance. And tears stung Lyddie's eyes. *Dawdi*'s beard used to ripple like that, except his came from laughter, not meanness. *Dawdi* had been bald too, and he couldn't get out of bed. And then. . .

"A-are you g-going to die?"

"Not right this minute, I don't think. Although the Lord may have other plans. No one knows the day or hour." He peered closely at her. "Are you crying?"

This time his question sounded softer, almost as if he cared. Lyddie risked peeking up at him, and he did look concerned. Now he looked even more like *Dawdi*. She blinked hard.

"What's wrong?" he asked.

He'd said it so gently, Lyddie answered, "You look like my *dawdi*."

"And that makes you sad?"

"He died."

The man sat silent for a moment. "I'm sorry." He hesitated a moment as if he didn't know what to say, then he asked, "I guess you miss him?"

Lyddie tried to choke back the sob, but it escaped, along with a mess of tears. The man motioned for her to sit on the chair by the bed. Then he pushed aside the water pitcher on the bedside table, reached for a small box of tissues, and handed her one.

She sniffled into the tissue and crumpled it in one hand. The other still held the ball of red construction paper. "I'm sorry."

"Don't be sorry about crying. Everyone needs to do it sometimes." He reached for a tissue himself and honked into it. "I would if I could," he mumbled.

His words made Lyddie curious. "Why can't you?"

His eyes filled with sadness, and she felt sorry for him.

He shrugged. "I try to be strong, but it's not always easy. Especially after someone you love dies."

She nodded. "Did your *dawdi* die too?"

"No, my wife."

"Oh."

He rubbed his forehead and looked as if he wanted to cry. "I miss her."

"I miss *Dawdi* too."

This time Lyddie wasn't afraid to meet the man's eyes, because he had tears in his, just like she did.

After a quick dab at his eyes, he handed her another tissue. She dropped the construction paper ball into her lap to reach for the clean tissue.

"Enough crying," the man announced.

His voice had gone crusty again, but now Lyddie wasn't afraid of him. Although she was still crying on the inside, she dried her tears and tried not to let sadness leak out of her eyes.

"You never did tell me why you came in here," he said.

"Oh." Lyddie fiddled with the construction paper ball. How much trouble would she be in for not doing her assignment?

Slowly, she uncrumpled the red paper. "I was hiding from my teacher."

He stared at her with shock in his eyes. "You ran away from school?"

"No." Lyddie explained about the assignment. Then she smoothed the wrinkled paper. "I was supposed to meet Mary Hess in the room next door." She swallowed hard. "I got scared and hid. Only I thought this was a broom closet."

"A broom closet?" He chuckled. "This looks like a broom closet to you?"

She shook her head. "It was dark, and there's a broom closet at the other end of the hall."

"You hide out in broom closets a lot?"

"No," Lyddie giggled. "*Mamm* works here, so I helped her by putting away the broom." She didn't want to hurt his feelings, but she should tell the truth. "I never would have come in here if I thought anyone was in here."

"I'm glad you did," he said quietly, so quietly Lyddie wasn't sure she'd heard him. But his eyes showed he was happy.

"I am too," she admitted, ducking her head.

"I guess we should introduce ourselves." He extended his hand. "I'm Moses Graber."

She shook his hand. "I'm Lyddie Chupp."

"You know, Lyddie, I'd rather hide out in my room than meet a stranger. I always kept to myself at home," Moses told her. "Being here"—he waved a hand toward the door of his room—"where people walk in and out all day is difficult."

"I wouldn't like that." She felt sorry for him being in a hospital with people around him all day. At least she could retreat to her room at home. And she didn't mind being around *Mamm*. Her mother was quiet.

"People walk in and out all day. And I don't like being helpless, depending on others to care for me. And—" He stopped and drew in a breath. "My son Daniel would scold me for complaining."

"But I won't," Lyddie whispered.

Moses lifted his head from the pile of pillows semi-propping him up. "Being here has made me into a cranky, old man."

Lyddie shook her head. She didn't think so.

Chapter Seven

As Fern pushed her patient back from physical therapy, she almost ran into Ruthie.

Wringing her hands together, Ruthie rushed up to her. "There you are. I've been looking all over for you."

"Is something wrong?" Fern kept heading toward Martin's room as Ruthie hurried along beside her.

"Lyddie's missing." The worry lines on Ruthie's face deepened. "Everyone's ready to go, but we can't find Lyddie."

"I don't understand." Fern had been sure Lyddie would be first in line to leave. She opened Martin's door, and Ruthie followed her into the room. Fern wished Ruthie would wait in the hallway, but Ruthie was frantic.

"She was assigned to Mary Hess. Lyddie took the sign off the door, so we assumed she was in the room."

"No one noticed she wasn't?"

"No, because the door was closed." Ruthie moaned. "It's all my fault. Darla wanted to open the door, but I explained about Lyddie's shyness. I thought maybe talking would be easier for her if, if"—she swallowed hard—"she had some privacy."

"And she didn't stay in the room with Mary?"

"She didn't even go into the room in the first place. Mary said she didn't see Lyddie at all."

So Lyddie had slipped off before she did her assignment? "I think I know where she might be." Fern assisted Martin into bed. "Let me get Martin settled, and then I'll check."

"*Ach*, that's such a relief. I'll go tell Darla."

"I apologize," Fern said to Martin as Ruthie rushed from the room.

"Is everything all right?" Martin asked. "It sounded like an emergency. If you need to help, please go right ahead."

"That's all right. My daughter's school is visiting here today." Fern straightened his sheet and blankets, moved the box of tissues, and poured him a glass of water. "It seems my daughter's gone missing. She's very shy and was dreading the visit. I'm pretty sure we'll find her hidden away somewhere, curled up in a chair, reading a book."

"A girl after my own heart. I preferred reading to talking when I was young." Martin chuckled. "You wouldn't guess that now, would you?"

Fern smiled. Usually, he was one of her most talkative patients. And despite being bashful, he'd gone on to be a minister in the Mennonite church. That made Fern hopeful that someday Lyddie would conquer her shyness.

She hurried from Martin's room and headed straight for the lobby and Lyddie's favorite chair. But the armchair was empty. Fern's heart sank. She'd been so sure she'd find her daughter here.

All the students, dressed in coats and bonnets, milled around near the outer door, while Ruthie and Darla roamed up and down the hallways, peeking into all the open rooms.

Where else might Lyddie hide? Fern checked the bathroom, the coatroom, the small library on the second floor, but no sign of her daughter.

What about the broom closet? Fern sprinted down the hall and yanked open the door. She turned on the lights to peer behind mops and buckets and pyramids of paper towels stacked on the floor. No Lyddie.

She had to be here somewhere.

Fern hurried back to the lobby. "I didn't find her."

Teary-eyed, Ruthie said, "I need to get the other children back to the schoolhouse for dismissal. Some of their parents will be waiting to pick them up."

"Go ahead, and don't worry about Lyddie. We'll find her."

Ruthie took Fern's hand. "I'm so, so sorry."

"No, I'm the one who should be apologizing. My daughter disobeyed your instructions."

"Please will you let me know when you've found her?" After Fern nodded, Ruthie motioned for all the scholars to line up, and they marched out the door.

Fern stood staring after them, so lost in thought, she didn't notice Daniel entering until he greeted her.

He studied her face. "You look upset. Is something wrong? Did the children not enjoy their visit?"

"The visits went well, all except one."

❄

"Not my *daed*, I hope," Daniel said.

A ghost of a smile flitted across Fern's face to be replaced with a look of concern. "*Neh*, your *daed* seemed, um, unenthusiastic about the program, so I didn't add his name to the list."

"That's good." Daniel slipped one arm out of his coat sleeve. "So what's the matter?"

"We lost my daughter."

Daniel froze. He was grateful he'd turned to free his other arm from the coat, so he was facing away when her blow hit. "Your daughter?" he asked in a strangled voice. He pretended to struggle with his coat to take some time to compose himself.

"Yes, Lyddie came with the rest of the scholars, but she didn't want to visit her assigned room because she's shy."

Lyddie? The little girl he met last night? The one who was so bashful she barely answered his questions?

Daniel took his time folding his coat over his arm to prevent her from seeing he was shocked. He'd made a terrible mistake. Because most Amish women stayed at home once they were married and had families, he'd assumed Fern was single. No wonder she'd dashed away last week.

Thinking about how he'd wandered the halls looking for her last Friday night made him so ashamed, he couldn't meet her eyes. But this wasn't about him.

"Can I help you find her? I know what she looks like."

"That's right. She mentioned you bought her some treats."

He'd also bought them for her mother. He hoped Fern would think he often bought snacks for people. Thursday she'd been hungry, so it made perfect sense. At least he hadn't found her on Friday night. But he had made a fool of himself earlier that day.

Shaking off the embarrassing thought, he asked, "Where have you looked so far?"

Before Fern finished ticking off the places she'd searched, the bright, bouncy Mennonite woman who led social programs at the rehab came barreling toward them. Daniel recognized her because she'd tried to interest *Daed* in several events. *Daed*'s clipped answers never hurt her feelings, and she always returned with more suggestions.

"Have you found her yet?" she asked.

Fern shook her head. "Not yet, Darla, and I need to get back to work. I skipped my lunch break to get ready for the children, so the time I've spent looking for Lyddie can count as my half-hour break."

"We did a thorough search of the second and third floors," Darla said, "Everyone knows to watch for her."

"Daniel offered to help." Fern gestured toward him.

"I'm happy to do whatever I can," he told her.

Darla turned her generous smile in his direction. She was a pretty girl, but her smiles didn't send his heart into overdrive the way Fern's did. Daniel caught himself. He had to stop thinking about her that way. His spirits plummeted.

"Why don't you search the dining room?" Darla suggested. "I'll check the employee locker room and kitchen downstairs."

Daniel started to watch Fern walk down the hall, then jerked his gaze away. He headed for the dining room. He felt foolish crawling around on his hands and knees to peer under tablecloths. He even checked under the decorative skirts of the buffet table and the round, ornamental tables scattered through the dining room and lobby. But whatever it took, they had to find Lyddie.

And searching for her kept his mind from his foolish mistake.

He met Darla back in the lobby. "You checked all the rooms on this floor?"

"All the ones with open doors. I don't want to disturb people who are napping."

"Any luck?" Fern asked as she passed by.

"Not yet, but I'm sure we'll find her," Daniel said. "Do you think it would be all right for us to tap on closed doors just to check?"

Fern glanced at the clock over the receptionist's desk. "It's getting close to suppertime. Most people may not mind if you wake them now." She started down the other hall, then stopped. "Except your *daed*. He was adamant that he didn't want to be disturbed."

Daniel laughed. "I don't think we need to check his room."

"I agree." The smile lines that formed around Fern's eyes softened her face and made her even more attractive. "If Lyddie were brave enough to go in—"

"*Daed* would have scared her and kicked her out."

The two of them shared a smile, but Daniel broke eye contact immediately.

❄

Fern tried not to care when Daniel turned away. She'd definitely hurt him by running away. He'd offered to search for Lyddie, but only because he was naturally a thoughtful and caring person. But he avoided eye contact and seemed eager to leave when she walked in his direction.

Shaking off her disappointment, she entered the room of her last PT patient for the afternoon. By the time she pushed Margaret's wheelchair into the hallway, Daniel was several doors down, tapping at one of the closed doors. Fern was grateful they were headed in the opposite direction so she didn't need to pass him again.

If he'd lost interest, that's what she wanted, wasn't it? Or maybe she'd built his kindness into something that never existed.

"Are you all right dear?" Margaret asked.

Startled, Fern realized she'd been staring down the hallway.

Margaret turned to look up Fern. "He's very good-looking, isn't he? And a very nice person. Not many sons would put up with a father like that."

"Yes, he is good to his *daed*." And to others.

Reaching up to pat Fern's hand, Margaret said, "I approve of your choice."

Fern gulped. "My choice? I don't think—"

"Oh, you can't fool me. I know young love when I see it."

"It's not like that," Fern protested. At least not on Daniel's part. And as for her, she'd made her decision. Falling in love was much too dangerous.

❄

Daniel went down one side of the hall and back up the other, knocking on every door. Every door except his *daed*'s. No one had seen Lyddie.

On impulse, he walked down the hall, calling her name. He had no idea if it would do any good, but if she was hiding, maybe she'd come out.

"Daniel?" *Daed*'s gruff voice called through the door as Daniel turned to head up the other side of the hallway. *Ach,* he'd woken *Daed,* and now he'd be in for it.

He'd rather wait for the confrontation, but *Daed* knew he was out here, so he'd better get this over with. He turned the knob, walked in, and stopped short.

Lyddie was sitting in the chair by the bed, smiling at *Daed*. Daniel rubbed his eyes. That must be a figment of his imagination. But when he looked again, he was even more surprised. *Daed*'s expression had softened.

"Lyddie, everyone's been looking all over for you."

She shrank back and lowered her eyes. "I-I'm sorry."

"Don't scare her," *Daed* barked, then he lowered his voice. "Can't you see she's shy and sensitive?" In his usual belligerent manner, he added, "What took you so long to get here tonight?"

"I was helping to look for Lyddie. The staff have all been searching for her. I joined in."

"*Ach!*" Lyddie jumped up from the chair. "I'm in big trouble."

Daniel stared at her. That was the longest sentence he'd ever heard her utter. "No, no. I don't think so. I'm pretty sure everyone will be relieved you've been found."

Daed puffed up like a barnyard rooster readying for a fight. "Anybody who tries to scold her will have to come past me first."

What was going on here? Lyddie talking? His *daed* defending her? If he didn't know better, he'd say he was dreaming.

"I'd better let people know you've been found." He hurried from the room and told Darla, who was draping the doorway in pine garlands.

She beamed. "Wonderful. I'll just finish hanging this mistletoe. Then I'll tell the rest of the staff."

"Do you know where Fern is?" Daniel asked her.

"I think she went down to pick up Margaret from PT."

Daniel sprinted to the elevator. "I'll go tell her." He pressed the button and waited impatiently for the slow moving machinery to crank from B to level 1. The door opened, and Fern stood there.

The minute their eyes met, a jolt ran through him. Had that been an answering expression in hers? Daniel shook his head and lowered his eyes. He kept forgetting.

"I told you so," Margaret said, a satisfied expression on her face, and Fern blushed a becoming shade of pink.

Not that Daniel noticed. Or at least, he tried not to notice.

"Daniel, what are you doing here?" Fern asked, her voice a little shaky.

"I, um." He suddenly realized he was blocking their exit. "I planned to take the elevator to find you." He stepped back so Fern could push the wheelchair into the hallway. "We found Lyddie."

"You did?" The stress lines around her mouth disappeared into a huge, relieved smile. "Where was she?"

"You wouldn't believe it if I told you. You'll have to see for yourself."

Fern shot him a quizzical look.

"I believe he's making excuses to spend time with you," Margaret said. "I just hope you don't plan to abandon me here in the hallway."

"Oh, no, I'd never do that," Fern said, although, until Margaret spoke, Fern had forgotten all about her. She'd been staring at Daniel. She loved how his eyes twinkled when he was keeping a secret, the way a slash of a dimple appeared in his cheek when he smiled, how he—

"Ahem," Margaret said, fake coughing to get Fern's attention. "I know I don't put stars in your eyes like—"

"So what's on the menu for dinner, Margaret?" Fern talked over the woman before she could finish her sentence.

Although Fern didn't know exactly what Margaret planned to say, it was guaranteed to be embarrassing. She'd already acted like Fern and Daniel were a couple. And she was determined to point it out.

Fern's first goal was to move Margaret out of Daniel's hearing range. Then once she had Margaret in her room, she could see Lyddie. And perhaps give her daughter a piece of her mind. After she hugged her, of course.

"Meet me at room twenty-two," Fern called over her shoulder to Daniel. "Please? I'm done with work at five." By the time she finished with Margaret, her shift should be over.

"I'll be waiting," he answered.

"Wasn't that a little forward, dear?" Margaret asked as Fern race-walked the wheelchair down the hallway. "And could you slow down a bit? I'm not planning to enter any NASCAR races at my age."

"Sorry." Fern slowed to a sedate pace. She hoped Daniel hadn't gotten the same meaning from her request as Margaret had. She'd only been excited to be reunited with her daughter again. At least, that's what she tried to tell herself. Her fluttering pulse told a different story.

"I'd been hoping for a shower before dinner," Margaret said as Fern pushed her over the threshold of the room.

Fern sighed inwardly. "All right." Helping Margaret shower would take at least half an hour. Then she'd need help dressing.

"Don't sound so disappointed, dear." Margaret flashed her a cheeky smile. "I said I'd been hoping. Not that I'd intended to take one. I certainly got the reaction I intended."

"I see." Trying to keep her expression neutral, Fern helped

Margaret onto the bed. But when she glanced up to see Daniel in the doorway, her heart sped up.

"*Yoo-hoo!*" Margaret waved a hand in front of Fern's face. "I'm over here. You can gaze at him as much as you want after you leave my room."

Hoping Daniel hadn't heard Margaret's statement, Fern turned her attention to the elderly lady. "Do you need anything else?" Fern asked.

"I do, but I don't want to keep you from your date."

"I'm happy to do whatever you need."

Margaret waved her away. "I was only teasing. Go ahead and leave."

With one last glance to be sure she hadn't left anything undone, Fern headed out the door to join Daniel.

"Ready?" he asked. When she nodded, he gestured down the hallway. "Right this way." He stopped before he reached his *Daed*'s door. "We're here."

"But the only other room is your *daed*'s."

"Then I suggest you peek in there."

Fern took a few steps forward until she was even with the door. Then she sucked in a breath. Lyddie was sitting on a chair beside the bed, talking to Daniel's *daed*. Tears filled Fern's eyes. If that wasn't a miracle. . .

"Surprised?" Daniel asked.

"Overwhelmed is more like it. I can't believe she's actually talking. And how did they get together?"

"That's what I'd like to know."

"Well, I guess the best way to find out is to ask." Fern walked into the room.

Lyddie stopped talking and turned to face her. "*Mamm?*" A guilty look crossed her daughter's face. "I, um, didn't do my assignment."

"So I heard. Do you know your teacher and everyone here on staff have been looking for you?"

"I'm sorry." Lyddie dipped her head and looked as if she were about to cry.

"I already told Daniel," Moses said, "I'm not going to let anyone scold her. Do you have any idea how frightened she was when she hid in my room?"

"Hid in your room?" Fern couldn't believe Lyddie would have run here to avoid talking to mild-mannered Mary Hess.

"Maybe you should let her tell you the whole story," Moses suggested.

Was Fern imagining it, or did Moses seem less cantankerous?

"You might want to take a seat," Moses said. "This may take a while."

Fern pulled a chair close to her daughter, and Daniel perched on the foot of the bed.

Lyddie began her story and described her fear, running away, mistaking Moses' room for the broom closet, and later talking to Moses. "And," she finished, "I guess it worked out all right, because I made a new friend."

"And so did I," Moses said.

Daniel's incredulous glance mirrored Fern's reaction exactly. Neither of them could ever have believed something like this even could have happened. The fact that it did was definitely a miracle. For both of them. If only God could work one more miracle and change her heart and Daniel's.

Chapter Eight

When Fern walked Lyddie to school the next morning, Ruthie rushed over and hugged Lyddie.

"I'm so glad to see you," Ruthie exclaimed. "What happened yesterday?"

"It's a long story. Maybe Lyddie would like to tell it to you on the playground today." Her daughter gave her a pleading look.

After Ruthie moved on to greet other scholars, Fern leaned down and said to Lyddie, "It will give you something to do." Much better for Lyddie than drifting around the edges of the playground and being left out of activities. "Plus, it's good for you to get more practice speaking to other people."

"I can't," Lyddie whispered.

"You most certainly can." Fern wasn't about to let Lyddie refuse to try scary new experiences. "If you made friends with Moses, believe me, you can make friends with anyone."

"But Moses was easy."

Fern shook her head. Most people would disagree. So many other people—adults and children—would gladly be friends with Lyddie, but her daughter had chosen a person the rest of the world would have difficulty loving.

"You might find other people will be easy too, if you give them a chance." Fern hugged her daughter good-bye. "I know it's hard for you, Lyddie, but please try."

Her daughter gave her a crooked smile—an *I-don't-believe-you,* nervous twist of her lips—that made Fern bend down and hug Lyddie again.

"Pray about it," Fern suggested. "God will help you."

And maybe it was time for Fern to do the same. She'd spent more time worrying than trusting.

While she walked to the center, Fern prayed, turning her concerns about Lyddie and Daniel over to the Lord. By the time she reached work, her spirits had lifted, and her heart felt lighter.

At ten o'clock, she went to Moses's room to take him to physical therapy. She greeted him, and instead of his usual grumbles or grunts, he surprised her by asking her a question.

"You know that program with the schoolhouse your daughter was doing yesterday?" he said as she assisted him into the wheelchair. "How do I sign up to participate?"

"I'll talk to Darla about it." Fern was positive Darla would welcome Moses with open arms. She'd been trying to get him to participate in programs since he arrived two weeks ago.

Worry lines formed on Moses's forehead. "Is it hard to get in?"

"Well, everyone's already been matched."

His lips turned down. "So I can't get Lyddie? If I can't get her, I'm not interested." He crossed arms over his chest.

"I'm not sure what to do about Mary Hess. She was supposed to be Lyddie's partner." Fern pushed Moses toward the elevator.

"But Lyddie's afraid to talk to Mary. That's why she ended up in my room."

Pressing the elevator button, Fern replied, "I know." She was torn between encouraging her daughter to get over her fears and protecting her from them. Maybe working with Moses could help her to overcome her fears. And Fern wanted to encourage this unlikely friendship because it appeared to be benefiting both Lyddie and Moses.

While they waited for the elevator, Fern mused, "I'm pretty sure Darla will agree, but Lyddie's teacher also needs to approve."

That afternoon when Lyddie arrived, she begged to be allowed to interview Moses for her assignment. Lyddie gazed up at Fern with pleading eyes. "Please?"

"I'll talk to Ruthie. She has to make the final decision." Darla had agreed earlier that day and offered to talk to Mary Hess. Fern had a feeling Ruthie would approve the switch. She and Ruthie both wanted to encourage Lyddie to come out of her shell. "Did you talk to Ruthie on the playground today?"

"Kind of." Lyddie scuffed the toe of her shoe on the tile floor and didn't meet Fern's eyes.

"What does that mean?"

"I tried, but the words got stuck in my mouth."

"Well, I'm not going to approve the switch until you tell Ruthie the whole story."

"*Mammmm...*"

Fern waved a hand to cut off Lyddie's whining tone. "I'm not changing my mind." Her daughter's deep, put-upon sigh would not affect the decision either.

"Is it all right if I visit Moses?" Lyddie asked.

"You must really like him."

"I do, *Mamm.* He understands me. And I understand him."

Despite their vast differences in age, the two of them seemed to have developed a close bond.

"You may visit him, but only if he wants company."

Lyddie skipped off down the hall. Today was the first time since their move from Ohio that Fern had seen her daughter happy or excited. *Please, Lord, let her continue to make friends and adjust to our new home.*

❄

Lyddie tapped lightly at the door. When Moses didn't answer, she turned the knob and tiptoed into the room.

Snores, wheezes, and grunts filled the air, and Lyddie giggled softly. Asleep, Moses sounded just like *Dawdi*. Closing her eyes, she imagined herself back in Ohio with *Dawdi*. The noises wrapped her in familiar comfort. She missed *Dawdi* so much.

"What are you doing?"

Moses loud question startled her from her memories. He'd asked the same question yesterday. Then she'd been shaking when she answered. Today she wasn't afraid of him.

"Remembering," she said. "Your snoring reminded me of my *dawdi*."

"I don't snore," he snapped.

Lyddie laughed. "Yes, you do."

Hmmph.

Moses sounded like he didn't believe her, but she'd told the truth. Maybe he was embarrassed. "*Mamm* said I needed to ask you if it was all right to spend time with you."

"I guess," he said grumpily. "Why would you want to do that?"

Tears welled in Lyddie's eyes. He didn't want her here. She'd thought they'd made friends yesterday.

"You're not going to start crying again?" Moses asked.

Lyddie hadn't planned to, but sometimes her eyes leaked. She didn't know how to stop them.

She should never have come in without asking. Maybe he'd only been kind yesterday because he'd felt sorry for her. She headed for the door.

"Where are you going?" His gruff voice stopped her in her tracks.

"Out to the lobby to read my book."

"Your teacher won't be upset if you don't do your assignment?" The touch of sarcasm in his tone hurt Lyddie's feelings.

"School's over today. Besides, we only do that program on Wednesdays."

"Why did you come then?"

Usually Lyddie didn't like to tell people her deeper feelings because she worried she'd say something wrong, hurt them, or make them dislike her. She didn't have to worry about that with Moses because it sounded like he already disliked her. A lot.

She whirled around and let the words boiling inside her spill out. "I came because I thought we were friends. I guess we're not." She spun back around before he could see the hurt in her eyes. Or the tears. She didn't know much about making friends, so maybe she'd been mistaken.

Shoulders slumped, she shuffled toward the door. Books made better friends. They never criticized you, hurt your feelings, or changed their minds.

"Stand up straight." Moses's voice cracked across the room. "Otherwise you might end up all hunched over when you're as old as me. And why are you sniveling?"

She drew herself up and straightened her spine. "I wasn't sniveling." At least she didn't think she had been. "I'm just disappointed."

"Disappointed not to spend time with me?" he asked, incredulous. "You really came in here to be with me?"

"That's what I said."

"And you meant it?"

Lyddie had reached the door. She turned the knob. "I don't lie."

"Wait," Moses said. "Look at me."

Reluctantly, Lyddie turned, but she couldn't bring herself to look him in the eye.

"Why would you want to spend time with a grumpy old man like me?"

"I already told you why."

"Because you like me and want to be friends?" He said it as if he didn't believe it was true.

Lyddie nodded. "Why else would I be here?"

"I thought your *mamm* or the school made you come in to cheer me up."

"I'm not a very good cheerer-upper. You should know that from yesterday."

"I don't know about that. You certainly made me happy yesterday."

"I did?" Lyddie nibbled on her lower lip. "Then why don't you want me to visit you today?"

"Because I didn't believe you'd want to spend time with me," he said miserably.

His reply puzzled her. "Why would you think that?"

Moses shrugged. "I'm a boring old man, so I figured someone was forcing you to keep me company. I care about you too much to keep you here when you'd rather be reading."

"I'd rather be with you than read."

His eyes widened. "You would? I've heard how much you like to read."

When she nodded again, he lowered his eyes and mumbled, "Sometimes you worry people might reject you, so you push them away before they hurt you."

That was true. Afraid the kids at school wouldn't like her, Lyddie had stayed away from them and refused to talk.

"Will you forgive me, Lyddie?" Moses asked. "And can we start this afternoon over again?"

"I'd like that."

Moses face brightened with a huge smile that reached his eyes. "Welcome, Lyddie. I'm pleased you came to see me today."

Wriggling with delight, Lyddie grinned back. "Hi, Moses. I'm happy to be here." Then she crossed the room and pulled the chair as close to his bed as she could, so she could talk to her new friend.

❄

The next morning Fern prodded Lyddie into leaving for school early. "I want to arrive before any of the other scholars. You need to tell Ruthie about Moses."

"Do I have to?"

Fern didn't answer. She only straightened Lyddie's safety vest, pulled on one of her own, and ushered Lyddie out the door.

Ruthie's eyebrows rose when they walked into the schoolhouse. She glanced at the clock. "You're early."

"Lyddie has something she'd like to ask you, but first I wanted her to explain about Wednesday."

"I see." Ruthie turned to Lyddie, who had her hands clenched in front of her. Her face was twisted up, as if she were trying hard not to cry.

Fern's heart ached for her daughter, but she refused to help her. Lyddie had to learn to speak up. Fern squeezed Lyddie's shoulder to show her support.

At first silence reigned. Then Lyddie spoke hesitantly, stopping and starting and backtracking. She explained about hiding in Moses's room, but when she got to the part about their conversation and friendship, her words flowed and her face shone.

When she finished, Ruthie appeared stunned. "Well, that's quite a story."

"That leads to Lyddie's question," Fern said. She patted her daughter's shoulder to give her courage.

Lyddie shot Fern a desperate look, pleading with her to ask. But this was her daughter's responsibility.

Stumbling over her words, Lyddie asked, "Could Moses be my partner?"

Although Ruthie gave a cautious *we'll see,* Lyddie clapped her hands and jumped up and down. Fern had never seen her daughter that excited. Evidently, neither had Ruthie.

"I guess this means a lot to her," Ruthie said after Fern convinced Lyddie to run out to the playground.

Fern's eyes grew misty. "I think this is her first real friendship outside the family."

Last night Daniel and Fern had arrived at the room to find Lyddie and Moses deep in conversation. With wonder in her eyes, Fern had turned to look at Daniel, only to find him gazing at her, bemused. She couldn't tell if his look was from seeing his *daed* so cheerful or if Daniel had been preoccupied with staring at her. He'd quickly shuttered his response and turned back to watch his *daed* and Lyddie.

On the walk home, Lyddie had turned to her. "*Mamm*, do you know why Moses is so grumpy?"

Fern had a few ideas, ideas she'd shared with Daniel, but she was curious to hear Lyddie's thoughts on the subject. "Why, Lyddie?"

"He's afraid people won't like him. At first he even tried to scare me off. But I'm glad I didn't let him."

Her daughter seemed to be learning valuable lessons about life and about getting along with people.

"You know, Lyddie, I think most people are scared of making friends because they worry the other person won't like them. They just show it in different ways."

"Moses said that too. He gets grumpy and mean. I'm scared to talk."

And I put on a smile to hide my fear, but it's there all the same. And sometimes it turned into awkwardness, stuttering, or even running away, like with Daniel.

❄

Daniel had gotten off work a little early tonight because he'd be doing a double shift tomorrow. The closer it came to Christmas, the longer the woodworking shop stayed open. They had so many orders to finish.

Daed might still be napping unless Lyddie had arrived to keep him company. Daniel smiled to himself. That little girl had somehow found a way to reach *Daed*'s heart. Although *Daed* still pretended to be gruff on the outside, Lyddie had exposed a hidden tenderness.

Like her *mamm*, she was a charmer. Fern had a gift for making people feel comfortable and happy. It seemed Lyddie had inherited the same talent.

Lost in thought, Daniel loosened his grip on the reins. His horse knew the way to the rehab center, and he'd plod along, making the correct turns. Ahead in the dimness of the overcast skies, a small girl skipped along.

Was that Lyddie?

She walked from school to the center every afternoon. Once before, he'd stopped to offer her a ride, but she'd turned him down, with a bowed head, a quick *neh*, followed by a soft *danke*. Maybe now that she knew him better, she'd accept.

He grasped the reins tighter to encourage his horse to pick up the pace. At a loud roaring in the distance, he tensed. A motorcycle blazed down the road. He'd wait until it passed.

The cycle screamed up the hill, the engine thundering. The driver swerved all over the road. Was he drunk?

It zoomed toward him. Daniel yanked the reins to steer the horse off the road and into the ditch. He gripped the leather until it bit into his hand to keep the horse from bolting.

The driver buzzed by, only inches away from the back of the buggy. Still shaking, Daniel watched in horror as the cycle veered to the other side of the road, then overcorrected and headed straight toward Lyddie.

"No!" Daniel screamed.

Lyddie half turned. She stood frozen in the beam of the headlight, her mouth open in an O.

The driver leaned into a quick turn to avoid her, but clipped her as he zoomed by. Lyddie flew into the air. Without stopping, the motorcycle zipped over the hill and out of sight.

Shaken and still breathing hard from his own near-accident, Daniel jumped out of the buggy and sprinted to where Lyddie lay, near the stubble of a chopped-down cornfield.

Dazed, she stared up at him. "Daniel?" she whimpered, "my leg hurts."

Daniel said a quick prayer of gratitude that she was conscious. And that she was breathing and talking. "Does anything else hurt besides your leg?"

"My back and my elbow. And I bumped my head."

"Don't try to move," he warned. Oh, how he wished he had one of the cell phones he'd joked about with *Daed*. He hated leaving Lyddie alone here to run to the rehab center, but he had to call an ambulance and let Fern know.

Lord, please help us.

Tears were dripping down Lyddie's cheeks, and she was shaking. Daniel took off his coat and draped it around her, being careful not to touch the leg or jar her back.

He set a hand on her head. "I need to—"

A car rumbled up the hill. Daniel jumped to his feet, rushed to the side of the road, and waved frantically.

The driver skidded to a stop a few feet beyond where Lyddie lay. He jumped out of his car. "What happened?"

"A motorcycle hit this little girl."

"I'll call 9-1-1." Whipping out his cell phone, the man hit some buttons and reported the hit-and-run. "I saw that motorcycle. It sped past me going about a hundred miles an hour. Wish I'd taken its license number and reported it."

He followed Daniel over to Lyddie. "Is she okay?"

"Her leg hurts, but she's awake and talking."

"That's always a good sign." He glanced from Daniel to Lyddie. "Your little girl?"

"No. Her mother works at the rehab. I should run over and let her know."

"I'll keep an eye on her," the man offered.

Daniel tried to stand, but Lyddie grabbed his hand. "Don't go."

"Seems like she'd prefer your company. Why don't I go over and tell her mother?" the man suggested.

"Her mom's name is Fern. Fern Chupp."

After checking both ways, the man dashed across the road and returned a short while later with Fern. She dropped to the ground beside Lyddie.

"Oh, Lyddie, what happened?"

Lyddie only shook her head, so Daniel explained. "An ambulance is on the way. I'm sure you'll want to go with her. If you give me your address, I can take your horse home and feed him."

"We don't have a buggy," Fern confessed. "We sold everything to move here."

No buggy? What kind of a husband would leave his family without transportation? No wonder she was working. "How do you get to the center? A driver? Do you need me to call to tell them?"

Fern shook her head. "We walk."

"From where?"

Fern waved vaguely over her shoulder. "Near town. About three miles or so from here."

That meant Lyddie did too. But with a broken leg, she'd never manage that distance.

An ambulance siren screamed in the distance, coming closer and closer. Fern shuddered as it drew up in front of them. Daniel wished he could offer some support. He stayed close to her as they stood and moved out of the way so the EMTs could examine Lyddie.

After Lyddie had been loaded in the ambulance, Fern got in, and the ambulance screeched away.

Daniel stared after it until it disappeared over the next rise.

Then he turned to the *Englischer* and shook his hand. "Thanks for your help."

"Any time. Hope the little girl will be okay."

So did Daniel. He whispered a prayer for Lyddie and for her *mamm*.

Chapter Nine

The next few hours flew by in a blur. X-rays, forms, consultations, signatures. Strange words flew at Fern. Tibia, fibula, ORIF, screws, plates.

She moved from curtained examining rooms to clanking elevators to waiting rooms with vinyl-cushioned chairs, blaring televisions, and glossy magazines.

Most of the time, Fern could be with Lyddie. Other times she couldn't. But wherever she was, poor Lyddie lay in the center of a revolving door of strangers. Nurses who questioned her, doctors who poked and prodded her, and aides who shuttled her from room to room.

After Fern had been reassured Lyddie's injuries were minimal, except for needing surgery on her leg, Fern worried about the bills. Ordinarily, the Amish community helped to cover them, but how could she ask them to do that when she'd only been to two church services?

Members of her Ohio community would volunteer, but she'd never ask them. Not after they'd just finished helping with her *daed*'s cancer expenses.

An even greater concern was holding onto her job at the rehab center. She hadn't even been at her job for a month yet, so she had no sick time. If she took off to care for Lyddie, she'd lose her position. Then how would she and Lyddie live and eat?

Lord, You promised never to give us more than we can bear, so I'm trusting You to heal Lyddie and take care of our financial concerns.

Fern pushed all her fears from her mind. God was in control, so she had no need to worry. Right now she needed to concentrate on taking care of Lyddie.

By the time the nurse called her back to talk to the doctor, a sense of peace flowed over her. Lyddie, her eyes scared and frightened, looked so small and fragile under the white sheets draped over her. Fern hurried over to her and took her hand.

"First of all, your daughter is a very lucky girl. It seems the motorcycle only grazed her. Most of her injuries are from being thrown into the air."

Fern sucked in a breath. "Most?"

"I didn't mean to alarm you. She has some cuts and bruises along with several brush burns. Her left leg bore most the impact of the landing. She broke both her tibia and fibula—the bones in the lower leg. I've scheduled surgery for tomorrow morning."

"What kind of surgery?"

"We'll use pins to hold the bone in place. Afterwards I'd like to keep her overnight for observation, but we can discharge her Sunday morning as long as everything goes well."

"I can spend the night with her?"

He nodded. "They'll be taking her to a room shortly." He looked over at Lyddie. "Good night, young lady. I'll see you in the morning."

After he left, Lyddie clung to Fern's hand. "Can we go home? I don't want to stay here."

"We have to, Lyddie. The doctor needs to fix your leg."

Fern stayed beside Lyddie as an aide took her to her room on the pediatric floor. A short while later, a light tap on the doorframe startled them. Daniel stood in the doorway, holding a balloon and two envelopes in one hand and a box in the other.

"Daniel!" Lyddie's beaming face revealed her excitement.

Fern tried to temper her own thrill at seeing him and forced herself to stay calm.

"*Daed* insisted I bring these to cheer Lyddie." He handed the small girl a box and tied the bright *Get-Well* balloon to the foot of her bed.

Lyddie opened the box. "Look, *Mamm*," she squealed, lifting several books from the box. "*Danke, danke!*" she said to Daniel after she'd examined the covers.

Lyddie's gushing thanks and exclamations over each book revealed her joy. What a thoughtful gift! Fern turned appreciative eyes toward Daniel. "You couldn't have given her a nicer present."

"I'm glad she likes them. I asked the salesperson at the Christian bookstore for recommendations. It seems she made great choices."

Fern lowered her voice so Lyddie couldn't hear her. "They'll be perfect for keeping her occupied before and after surgery."

"Surgery?" Daniel's brows drew together.

In a whisper, she explained Lyddie's injuries.

"I'm sorry to hear about the surgery, and I'll be praying for her full recovery." He held up the envelopes. "I forgot these." He handed one to Lyddie and the other to Fern.

"For me?" Fern asked. When he nodded, she opened the envelope, but paused when Lyddie giggled.

"Moses made me a card." She opened it so they could see a rough sketch of a man and a girl sitting in wheelchairs next to each other. Then she hugged it to her chest. "I'm going to keep this forever and ever."

Daniel smiled at her. "I'll tell *Daed* you liked it."

Fern pulled a notecard from her envelope. The floral design had a verse in the center:

Now faith is the substance of things hoped for, the evidence of things not seen. ~Hebrews 11:1

A folded piece of paper obscured the handwritten note inside. She lifted the paper to find a message from her supervisor, signed by everyone on duty that night:

Fern,

We're lifting you and your precious daughter in prayer. Martha has volunteered to take your shift tomorrow. Enclosed is a small gift to help you during Lyddie's recovery.

Fern opened the paper and frowned. No, that couldn't be right.

❄

"Is something wrong?" Daniel asked anxiously. Fern appeared to be on the verge of tears.

Her eyes moist, she said in a dazed voice, "I can't believe this." She held up a printout. "I just started working, so I can't take time off." In a voice clogged with tears, she said, "Ten people on staff volunteered to give me one of their sick days. I went from zero to ten sick days."

"*Mamm?*" Concern in her eyes, Lyddie stared at Fern.

"Your *mamm*'s fine, Lyddie," Daniel assured her. "She just got a special present."

"Then why's she crying?"

"Those are happy tears." And probably tears of relief. She had to be worried about her job. All those extra days would also allow her to take Lyddie to appointments.

An aide bustled into the room. "Will you and your husband both be staying the night?" she asked Fern.

"Husband?" Fern asked, her eyes still dazed.

"I'm a friend," Daniel corrected.

The aide's cheeks reddened. "I'm sorry." She gestured toward their Amish clothing. "I just assumed—"

Daniel smiled to put her at ease. "It's an understandable mistake. I just stopped by to bring a few gifts."

"I see." The aide turned to Fern. "Will your husband be joining you later then?"

Daniel's stomach clenched. He needed to get out of here before her husband arrived. He wasn't sure he could stand to see the man lucky enough to be married to Fern.

"No, I'm afraid not," Fern said. "He's—"

"My *daed*'s dead," Lyddie informed her.

"Oh, I'm so sorry." The aide's cheeks flushed again. "I didn't mean to—"

The aide wasn't the only one who was flustered. Daniel was scrambling to make sense of the shifting kaleidoscope as all the pieces fell into totally different and unexpected patterns.

Daniel barely heard the rest of the conversation while his brain tried to process the thought echoing in his mind. She was a widow.

"It's all right," Fern tried to reassure the aide. "You couldn't have known."

"I hope it wasn't recent," the aide said gently.

Her eyes sad, Fern gazed off into the distance. "No, it happened when Lyddie was two."

Daniel's admiration for her increased. She'd raised Lyddie on her own for the past seven years? The community would have helped, but it was still a heavy burden.

Why hadn't she remarried? A woman as beautiful as Fern must have had many offers. She'd mentioned nursing her *daed*. Maybe she'd had no time to date.

His thoughts flew back to her words at the scene of the accident. She had no buggy because they'd sold everything to move here. The community would help to pay Lyddie's hospital bills, but maybe he could organize a fundraiser.

Daniel wished he could stay longer, especially now that he

knew the truth about Fern, but Lyddie's eyes were drooping. And Fern needed her rest. Tomorrow would be a stressful day.

"I'd better be going," he said. "What time is Lyddie's operation tomorrow morning?"

"Eight." Fern nibbled at her lip, an anxious expression on her face.

"I'll be praying."

"*Danke* for everything," Fern whispered. She glanced at her daughter. "Please tell your *daed* how much Lyddie appreciates her card."

"I will." Daniel's lips curved up. "He'll be honored to know she plans to keep it forever."

❄

Fern tossed and turned most of the night. She woke early and slipped out of the room to wash up as best she could and grab a quick breakfast before Lyddie woke. Her daughter wouldn't have anything to eat until after surgery.

When she returned, Lyddie was just waking. She glanced around with sleepy eyes. "Where are we?"

"The hospital. You hurt your leg. Do you remember?"

Lyddie gazed at the balloon with a wide smile. "Daniel brought that. Where's my card from Moses?"

Fern had pried it from Lyddie's hands last night after she'd fallen asleep. "Right here." She lifted it from the bedside table.

Lyddie clutched it to her. "I'm keeping this with me."

"If they'll let you. You must do whatever they say."

A nurse entered the room. "Time for prep."

Fern followed as Lyddie was taken down for surgery.

"I'm scared, *Mamm*," Lyddie whispered as they prepared her for the operation.

Leaning close, Fern said a quiet prayer before her daughter

drifted off. She continued praying as she made her way to the waiting room where she'd hear the results of Lyddie's surgery.

She pushed the door open and stopped. Daniel sat in one of the green vinyl chairs with metal arms. As soon as he saw her, he rose and crossed the room.

He studied her face. "How are you doing?"

"I'm shaking," she admitted, with a nervous laugh.

"Come sit down." He led her to a quiet spot in the back of the room. "Waiting's the hardest part. Once she's out of surgery, you'll be able to relax."

"*Danke* for coming." Fern had been dreading sitting here for however long it took. She thanked God for sending someone as thoughtful as Daniel to keep her company.

❄

Daniel settled into the chair beside Fern, his heart thumping at being so close to her. After last night's bombshell, excitement filled him as he considered future possibilities, but now was not the time to think of those. His job here was supporting Fern.

He'd done this waiting alone during *Daed*'s surgery, and he didn't want Fern to experience that loneliness. He'd called the rehab center from the hospital last night and asked them to tell *Daed* his plans. Surely *Daed* would approve. Especially if it involved Lyddie.

Beside him, Fern clutched the metal chair arm, her fingers clenched and unclenched. Daniel had been through this, so he understood and sympathized with her anxiety.

Trying to comfort her, he slipped his hand over hers. He'd intended to soothe her. Instead, the softness of her small hand sent a shock through him. He longed to stroke her fingers, but he kept his hand steady.

"Do you think she'll be all right?"

"I'm sure she will be." He patted her hand. "Try not to worry."

"What if something happens to her? How will I go on?" Fern turned her hand over and clung tightly to his.

Daniel warned himself her movement had been a reflex, an unconscious reaction. She'd needed something to grasp. The same way she'd clutched the arm of the chair. But it took him a moment to come up with a coherent answer.

"Lyddie will be fine. It's routine surgery." He continued murmuring soothing words until her tense shoulders relaxed.

"I know it's silly to worry, but she's all I have left in the world."

"I understand. And she's a very special girl."

The grateful glance Fern gave him made his neck heat. He squeezed her hand lightly and ran a finger under his collar to release some of his nervous tension.

Holding hands with her seemed so right, so natural, so easy. He wished it had been under different circumstances. Even more, he wished he had the right to clasp her hand like this all the time.

❄

Daniel's touch comforted Fern, but it also sent a strange tingling up her arm. The sensations warmed her face as well as her heart.

If she hadn't been so concerned about Lyddie, Fern might have enjoyed it more. But she sat on the edge of her chair, ready to jump up the minute they called her name.

"Why don't you sit back and relax? This might take a while."

Daniel's gentle advice made sense, but how could she calm down when Lyddie was in surgery? "I wonder how long it will take."

"*Daed's* surgery lasted four hours, but—"

"Four hours?" Fern's voice edged into hysteria.

"His was a complicated break, which is why he's been in rehab so long. Plus, at his age, bones are more fragile. Lyddie's young and strong and healthy. I'm sure her operation won't take nearly as long."

She should have asked the doctor how long it would take. Maybe they wouldn't give an estimate in case they ran into problems. She only hoped they wouldn't take four hours. She wasn't sure she could last that long.

Fern had forgotten about Moses's operation. "Was it hard for you to wait while your *daed* was in surgery?"

"Very," Daniel admitted. "I was also lonely. Those hours were some of the longest of my life."

"I can imagine. But didn't friends come to sit with you?" Whenever her *daed* had cancer treatments or when he started slipping away, she'd been surrounded by her supportive community.

"*Daed* fell in the middle of the night. He got up to get a drink of water and tumbled down the stairs. I didn't want to contact anyone at three in the morning."

"That's understandable." Fern was grateful not to sit here alone. "I really appreciate you being here with me. It helps to have company."

Over the next two hours, Daniel asked Fern about her life in Ohio, why they moved to Ephrata, and how they were settling in. She, in turn, learned he'd spent the past seventeen years caring for his *mamm* as her health deteriorated with rheumatoid arthritis and helping his aging *daed* take care of their small farm, while working full time at a woodworking business in town. Now he was looking after his *daed*.

With all his responsibilities, Fern wondered, but wouldn't dare ask, if he'd found time for courting. Or if he had a sweetheart now.

They were deep in conversation about losing a parent in the past six months, when Fern's name was called. Reluctantly letting go of his hand, she jumped to her feet and hurried over.

"Everything went well, and your daughter is doing fine," the surgeon assured her. "I put in two pins. You can see them on this x-ray." He held out a paper with a grayish image and pointed to two spots. "Here and here."

Fern nodded and tried to follow his explanations about the surgery, but her mind was only on one question: *When can I see Lyddie?*

Finally, he ended his monologue, and Fern let out her breath in a *whoosh*. Then taking a deep breath, she asked, "How soon can I see her?"

"She's in recovery now, but she should be back in her room within an hour or so."

Another hour? How could she possibly wait that long?

After the surgeon left, Daniel came up behind her. "Is anything wrong? You look upset."

Fern blinked back tears. "I can't see Lyddie for an hour."

"That's normal. They need to monitor her until the anesthesia wears off." Daniel took her elbow and steered her out of the waiting room. "Why don't we get some lunch in the cafeteria and then go up to the room to wait?"

His calming presence and words soothed her. But the touch of his fingers on her elbow burned through her. She should pull away, but she enjoyed being so close to him. So connected.

Maybe if she hadn't been so concerned about Lyddie, she'd be able to fight off her attraction. But fear for her daughter had lowered her guard. And somehow Daniel had snuck in past her defenses.

Chapter Ten

Fern appreciated Daniel distracting her over the next hour. They had a quick lunch and then hurried to the hospital room in case Lyddie returned early.

"Will you be all right if I run out to make a phone call?" Daniel asked. "I'm sure *Daed* would like to know the operation went well."

"Of course." Fern was still a little shaky, but the closer it came to Lyddie's return, the more excited she got. She'd miss Daniel's presence, though.

"I won't be long." He headed for the door. "Of if you'd rather have time alone with Lyddie, I can wait in the lobby."

"No, I want you to come back." As soon as she said it, Fern wished she could retract her words. She hadn't meant to give voice to the longing deep within her heart. "I mean," she stumbled, "I appreciate your conversation. It's helped to keep my mind off the waiting."

Once he was gone, Fern paced the room, watched the clock, and *rutsched* in the chair until Daniel returned.

"*Daed* was thrilled to hear the news. He said he'd been praying all morning."

"That's sweet of him."

Daniel laughed. "I think he's sweet on your daughter." He sobered for a minute. "I know he wishes he had a grandchild."

And Lyddie missed having her grandfather. Maybe that's why the two of them got along so well.

"By the way, while I was on the phone with the rehab center, I spoke to the director, and they've agreed to let you borrow one of the small portable wheelchairs," Daniel told her. "Lyddie can't possibly manage crutches for her walk to school."

"Oh, thank you." Fern suppressed the urge to hug him. "I hadn't even thought about that." She'd been too busy worrying about Lyddie's surgery to even think about how they'd manage once they got home.

"You're welcome," Daniel said. "But you're not going to push her to school every day."

Fern's head snapped up at his stern command. Of course, she was. She had no other way to get there. She couldn't afford to pay a driver.

All the words died on her lips when she met his eyes. The tenderness and caring in his gaze touched a place deep inside. A dark place where she'd stored all her anguish. Her fear. Her determination never to love again. And the floodgates came tumbling down.

Floodwaters poured out. All the emotions she'd denied threatened to overwhelm her. Helpless against the flow, she struggled to tune into what Daniel was saying.

"I don't want to think about you struggling uphill with a wheelchair," he insisted. "I'll pick you up in the morning and take you home after work. I can also get Lyddie after school and bring her to the center."

Still drowning in the surging water, Fern had to hold her ground before she was swept away—by the tidal waves and by Daniel.

The rational part of her mind warned she couldn't let him do this. Fern managed to shake her head. "I don't. . ."

Daniel held up a hand to stop her protest. "Most of those streets have no sidewalks. Do you know how horrible it was for me to stand there helpless and watch that motorcycle plow into Lyddie?"

At the look of horror on his face, Fern pushed past her swirling emotions to reach out to him. She wanted to smooth the lines on his face, comfort him, erase the terrible memories. Seeing Lyddie lying on the ground had been a heart-stopping moment. Fern couldn't imagine how awful it would have been to experience the moment of impact.

Daniel squeezed his eyes shut for a moment. When he opened them, he looked straight at her, his expression filled with caring. "I couldn't bear it if either of you got hit."

Those heartfelt words melted Fern's resistance. She was powerless to say no to his request. "All right," she whispered.

❄

Bottles clinked and wheels squeaked in the hallway, and Daniel stepped back to let a young man push Lyddie's bed into the room. She lay so pale and still, he sucked in his breath. A vivid memory of her flying through the air and landing on the ground flashed through his mind.

Then Lyddie's eyelashes fluttered. Daniel's breath leaked out in a long, slow hiss. She was alive. For a minute there, he'd wondered.

"Lyddie!" Fern's plaintive cry tore through him. She rushed to her daughter's side and bent down to hug her.

"Excuse me, ma'am," the young man said. "Can we get her situated first? Then you can spend as much time as you'd like with her."

Once Lyddie was tucked in, Fern drew a chair up to the bed

and took her daughter's hand and stared raptly at her. "She's blinking. Lyddie, can you hear me?"

The young man turned to Daniel. "Sir, can I explain about your daughter's IV and pain meds?"

His daughter. Oh, how Daniel wished it were true. Last night, he'd been mistaken for Fern's husband. And today, Lyddie's *daed*.

"Sir?"

"What?" Daniel came back to reality with a thud.

"The IV and pain meds?"

"Right. Of course." Even if he wasn't Lyddie's *daed*, he could explain it all to Fern later. He listened carefully to the instructions.

"And you'll be spending the night?" the young man asked.

"No, but her *mamm* will."

He sighed. "Then I guess I'd better repeat everything to her."

"No need," Daniel said. He hated to disturb Fern, who sat murmuring to Lyddie and watching intently for any flicker of movement. "I can tell her." When the young man looked as if he planned to protest, Daniel said, "My *daed* was in here two weeks ago with a broken hip. Things are slightly different for kids, but not too different. We'll be fine."

"If you're sure?" At Daniel's nod, he asked, "You know where the call button is?"

When Daniel pointed it out, the young man said, "Sorry. I didn't mean to be so grumpy. I was supposed to be off four hours ago, but we're short-staffed. And I missed lunch."

Daniel waved a hand. "Don't worry about it." He'd gotten used to *Daed*'s moods. This was nothing. "Hope you get to eat soon."

"I'mmm. . .sleepy," Lyddie slurred.

The joy on Fern's face made Daniel's heart pound so hard his chest ached.

"That's all right, baby," Fern told her. "You can sleep if you want to."

"I. . .feel. . .funny."

Fern leaned over and smoothed a few wayward curls back from Lyddie's damp forehead. "They put you to sleep to fix your leg."

Unsure whether he should go or stay, Daniel stood watching them until Fern beckoned him closer.

"Why don't you bring the other chair over here?" She indicated a spot beside her.

Daniel did as she asked. He debated a minute, then took Fern's hand. She smiled but didn't look at him, so he continued to hold it while she held one of Lyddie's hands. All three connected. Just like a real family.

❄

Lyddie woke before dawn and struggled to sit up, but her leg seemed to be stuck inside a heavy block. She closed her eyes again. Maybe she was dreaming. Strange sounds surrounded her —ticking, whooshing, clinking, even light breathing.

She rubbed her eyes and turned toward the breathing. Peeking through metal bars, she blinked until everything came into focus. Shadows striped the wall and *Mamm*'s face. *Metal bars? Strange room? Mamm sleeping beside her?* Slowly, it all came into focus. The hospital. She'd broken her leg.

Reaching tentative fingers under the covers, she ran her fingers over the block on her leg. Not a block, a cast.

Her mother let out soft whimpers, like she was crying in her sleep.

"*Mamm?*" she whispered.

Her *mamm* jerked awake. "Lyddie? Do you need something?"

Lyddie's leg was on fire, and her body ached in many different places, but all she wanted was for *Mamm* to hold her close. She held out her arms, and *Mamm* scooted up on the bed beside her and wrapped Lyddie in a tight hug.

❄

Grateful it was an off-Sunday, Daniel came to take them home in the early afternoon. While Fern signed papers, an aide helped Lyddie into a wheelchair. Lyddie clutched her balloon and card in one hand and held the stack of books with the other. Together they rode the elevator to the first floor. Like they were a family. Daniel wished he could hold Fern's hand again, but she stood on the other side of Lyddie's wheelchair.

When they reached the curb, Fern glanced around. "Where's the buggy?"

"I thought a car would be more comfortable for Lyddie. She can sit in the front seat and stretch out her legs."

Fern's eyes filled with tears. "I don't have enough money with me."

"You don't need to pay." Before she could protest, Daniel held up a hand. "*Daed* wanted to do this for Lyddie. It's to thank her for making him so happy."

Lyddie's eyes shone. "Moses is so nice."

Daniel smiled to himself. He'd like to take a poll at the nursing home to see how many people shared that opinion.

He helped Lyddie into the car, then climbed in the backseat beside Fern. She clasped her hands in her lap. From nervousness? Or was she trying to prevent him from holding her hand?

Once they reached Fern's house, Daniel took the folding wheelchair and a small pair of crutches from the trunk.

Fern's eyebrows rose. "You think of everything."

"I figured you might need them today, so I stopped by to pick them up before I came for you."

He handed the crutches to Fern and then lifted Lyddie into the wheelchair. He started wheeling her toward the front door, but stopped when Fern beckoned to him.

"Over here." She walked around the house to a side entrance. "We're renting two rooms over here." She dipped her head as if embarrassed, but then she straightened her spine, unlocked the door, and held it open so he could push Lyddie inside.

As soon as he entered, he understood Fern's concern about paying for a driver. The rooms were clean but sparsely furnished. He also understood why she didn't have a buggy. Even though the church would assist with Lyddie's bills, Daniel had an idea of how he could help too.

"Where do you want me to put you, Lyddie?" he asked.

She pointed to a bed.

"You're still tired?" He lifted her up and set her gently on the bed.

Fern bustled over with an extra pillow to prop her up. After Lyddie sank back against the pillows, her stack of books beside her, Fern walked him to the door.

She peered up at him shyly through her lashes. "*Danke*. For everything."

Fern probably had no idea how appealing she was when she did that. Daniel wanted to take her into his arms, but he jammed his hands into his pockets to prevent himself from reaching out. "I'd better go. I don't want to keep the driver waiting. What time should I pick you up tomorrow?"

"Lyddie and I start at eight thirty. I drop her off five or ten minutes early." A pained expression crossed Fern's face. "I don't want to cause any trouble for you. I can manage the wheelchair."

"No, I'm going to pick you up, at least for the next week or two." Longer than that if he she'd let him.

The determined set of Fern's jaw made it clear she didn't want to cooperate.

"I'll be here in plenty of time to get you to the schoolhouse," Daniel assured her. "Please don't start walking. I couldn't bear to think of either of you being in an accident. Promise me you won't?"

When her eyes softened and she nodded, Daniel fought the urge to enfold her in his arms. Right now, he didn't have that right. First, he needed to get up the courage to admit his true feelings.

❄

By the end of her first week home, Lyddie could hobble around on her crutches, but the wheelchair was easier. She could propel it herself if she had to, but it took a lot of work, and muscles she didn't normally use ached afterwards.

Daniel drove them to the schoolhouse every morning and picked her up in the afternoon. Lyddie spent time with Moses every day, but she still dreaded the writing assignment. She had no idea what to write about her partner.

Ruthie gave them time to write at school, but Lyddie crossed out more than she wrote. Because she hadn't finished in class, the night before the essay was due, she spent the whole evening working on it at home. She wasn't sure it was what her teacher had in mind, but when she recopied her final draft neatly, she felt like she had captured her time with Moses.

But the next morning, instead of collecting their essays, Ruthie clapped her hands for attention. Everyone fell silent.

"You've had a few days now to write your reports about your friends at the center," she said. "Now we're going to present them. I'd like you to come up front and read what you've written."

The oatmeal Lyddie had for breakfast churned in her stomach, turning into a rock-hard ball. She couldn't do this. If Ruthie made her read her essay to the class, she'd throw up.

Lyddie couldn't pay attention as the first graders read a few short, babyish sentences. Ruthie had let them draw pictures too, so they turned their papers around to show everyone. If only their reports weren't so short. They had barely taken any time, so Lyddie's turn was drawing closer.

The second graders went next. They only had to write three simple paragraphs.

Then it was time for the third graders. There were only two of them. Matthew and Lyddie. Ruthie turned to Matthew, who bounded to the front of the room and read his required page. As soon as he returned to his seat, Ruthie motioned to Lyddie.

The dread that had been building while each person read now glued Lyddie's tongue to her mouth and her body to her wheelchair. She couldn't do this. She just couldn't.

"Lyddie, it's your turn," Ruthie said gently. "Come on up here."

The only thing Lyddie could move were her eyes. And she used them to beg Ruthie not to make her go up front.

Her teacher's gaze grew sympathetic. Then she glanced at the paper on Lyddie's desk. "You wrote your report, didn't you?"

Lyddie managed a nod, but it set her stomach roiling. She'd filled the whole page and even had a few sentences on the back of the paper. She hoped she wouldn't get in trouble for writing more than the teacher had assigned. And she'd followed all the instructions, including ending with a lesson she'd learned from her friend.

"Come on up." Ruthie smiled to encourage her.

Lyddie pointed to the wheelchair, hoping it would serve as an excuse.

"Oh, you want some help?" Ruthie looked surprised because Lyddie had been propelling herself around the classroom earlier.

"Matthew?" Ruthie selected the oldest boy in the back of the room. "Could you please push Lyddie up front?"

Frantically, Lyddie shook her head. She hadn't meant for someone else to push her. But before she could protest, Matthew had grabbed the wheelchair handles and started toward the front of the room. He turned the wheelchair so Lyddie faced her classmates. Then he stepped to the side of the room to wait until she was done.

Lyddie held up her paper, trying to hand it to her teacher, but Ruthie shook her head.

Setting a hand on Lyddie's shoulder, she glanced down at

Lyddie's essay. "It looks like you've written a full page. Your classmates would like to hear it."

Lyddie's whole body shook. The paper rattled in her shaky hands. The writing on it blurred, and her teeth clamped too tightly to say a word.

Every eye in the classroom focused on her, and Lyddie thought she would die. She closed her eyes and bowed her head. *Please, Gott,* she begged, *please don't make me do this.*

Her paper fluttered from her nervous fingers and floated two rows back. Mary Elizabeth jumped up and brought it to the front of the room. She held it out to Lyddie, whose hands were clenched in front of her. Lyddie shook her head. She couldn't reach out to take the paper.

"Thank you, Mary Elizabeth," Ruthie said, taking the essay. "Why don't I read this today, Lyddie? Next time, though, I'll expect you to participate."

Lyddie wished she could be back in her seat instead of in front of all those staring eyes. She barely had time to whisper a *danke* to *Gott* before Ruthie started reading:

Leave Me Alone

By Lyddie Chupp

It's hard being shy. Everyone else enjoys meeting other people. They play together. They talk together. They laugh together.

But shy people get a sick feeling when they have to talk. Their stomachs hurt. Their hands shake. Their mouths get dry. All their words stick inside their mouths.

My friend at the rehab is Moses Graber. He is shy like me. He doesn't like being at the rehab center. It makes him grumpy.

I was scared of Moses at first. He had a deep, mean voice. It made me jump. I wanted to run.

At first he yelled, "Leave me alone."

But I had to stay. Sometimes if you stay with shy people without talking, they get more comfortable. But don't stare. They don't like that.

I sat and waited. I didn't talk and didn't stare. It was hard for both of us. We didn't know what to say.

Now we do. We can talk together. Sometimes we're just quiet. It's all right not to talk. We both like silence.

I learned making friends is easier when someone understands you and you understand them.

"Oh, Lyddie." Ruthie squeezed her shoulder. With tears in her eyes, she said, "Class, this is a good reminder that God created everyone different, and we need to respect those differences."

Giving Matthew a quick wave to let him know he could return Lyddie to her desk, Ruthie continued, "I hope everyone learned that as they made friends with their partners at the center." Ruthie waited until Matthew had pushed Lyddie back to her seat and then said, "Thank you for a beautiful essay, Lyddie."

All the stiff parts of her relaxed, and Lyddie's whole body melted into her wheelchair like soft candle wax. She barely heard the rest of the readings. Her heart sang. Ruthie had liked her essay, and Lyddie's time in the spotlight was over.

When Ruthie handed back the essays at the end of the day, she'd placed grades at the top of each essay. Lyddie couldn't wait to tell Moses the good news. The two of them had gotten an *A*.

Chapter Eleven

The more time she spent around Daniel, the harder Fern fell for him. Riding in the buggy with him every morning and evening was a tiny slice of heaven. And he won her admiration by treating Lyddie with great care, lifting her in and out of her wheelchair, talking to her about her schoolwork and reading, and acting like a father to her.

When they arrived at the schoolhouse, Daniel insisted on taking Lyddie inside. Her shy daughter soon warmed up to him. She even talked to him when he picked her up at school to transport her to the rehab center. Fern marveled at how much Lyddie had changed—at least around Moses and Daniel. But her daughter still had trouble speaking at school and conversing with other adults.

Fern's heart beat faster whenever Daniel and Lyddie arrived in the afternoon. Fern timed her fifteen-minute break so she could walk beside Daniel and Lyddie to Moses's room. Her daughter beamed and chattered excitedly as Daniel pushed her wheelchair down the hall. And Moses's brilliant smile when Lyddie arrived warmed Fern from head to toe.

Although Moses still grumbled at the staff, he'd lost much of his belligerence. Fern had to credit her daughter with that miraculous change. With Lyddie occupying Moses's time every afternoon, Daniel accompanied Fern while she worked. She treasured her time with him but missed the handholding they'd done at the hospital. He seemed to be keeping his distance from her.

One thing that puzzled her, though, was how every patient knew and greeted Daniel by name. Several times he hung back and talked to Martin, Margaret, and a few of the others, but they stopped speaking whenever she came near enough to hear.

"What were you two talking about?" Fern asked after Daniel stopped to talk to Martin a second time that evening.

A secretive smile crossed Daniel's face but disappeared so quickly Fern wasn't sure she'd seen it. "Martin's excited about the auction and yard sale this weekend. His church is going to be participating."

"Everyone's been talking about it. Even Lyddie. She wants to come to work with me on Saturday so she can attend."

Daniel smiled. "I can watch her, so you can work. I'm sure *Daed* would love to have her company. He seems as enthusiastic about it as she is."

Fern smiled. "And how do you plan to push two wheelchairs?" Lyddie was using her crutches more, but she tired quickly. She wouldn't be able to walk for long.

"I hadn't thought about that." He laughed. "I'll figure it out somehow."

By the time Saturday came, the whole rehab center was abuzz with excitement.

As Daniel drove past the schoolhouse, Lyddie squealed and bounced in her seat. "Look!" she pointed to the cars and buggies filling the parking area and lining the road.

Multi-colored balloons, tied to trees and fence posts, bobbed in the air. The balloon trail led to the rehab center, with an equally full parking lot. Large banners hung from the roofs of both buildings announcing the auction and sale. Despite the cold weather, people milled about the grounds where tents were set up.

Daniel and Lyddie planned where they'd go first. Hot chocolate and funnel cakes topped their list, followed by the petting zoo. Fern wished she could join them rather than going in to work.

Darla greeted her at the door. "Quite a few of our patients are eager to attend the sale. If you don't mind being out in the cold, we've selected you and Martha as the staff members who'll transport them."

"I don't mind at all." In fact, Fern was thrilled. She could not only be part of the fun, she could spend more time with Daniel and Lyddie.

"Great!" Darla handed her a list. "Here are the people and the times they've requested. Margaret has been very insistent she has to be in the auction tent at ten of two. They'll be auctioning a quilt she wants to buy."

Fern glanced at her list. No point in taking off her coat and bonnet. Martin had requested to be taken outside at eight. She'd better get him now.

Martin beamed when she walked through the door. "I was praying you'd get here early. I want to be in my church's booth today."

"How long will you be staying?" Fern asked.

"I hope I can make it all day, but if it's too painful, I'll have someone bring me back to the room." He handed her a small hand-drawn map with one spot circled. "Darla said this is where they're set up."

Fern pushed him down the outer ramp and onto the dried grass. Bumping over ruts and uneven ground, she managed to steer him to the booth he wanted. All the people in the booth came rushing out to greet him.

"Have a cup of hot chicken corn soup," he urged Fern. "Our church ladies make the most delicious recipe."

"Not now," she demurred. "But I promise to stop by at lunchtime."

"You do that," Martin said. "Your soup will be free. It's one small way I can thank you for your kindness in caring for me."

When Fern protested, he said, "I'll be doing it for all the rehab staff, but you're special."

She thanked him and hurried back toward the building. Daniel stopped her. He held two steaming cups and thrust one into her hand. "I know you have to work, but I want you to stay warm."

"Where are Lyddie and Moses?"

Daniel pointed to the small petting zoo, where a baby goat nuzzled Lyddie's hand. A tall boy stood behind Lyddie, holding the wheelchair handles.

Fern turned to Daniel in surprise. "Who's that pushing Lyddie?"

"Andrew, one of the boys from her school. He offered to help. Said he sits beside her at school, and he'd pushed her before."

Lyddie had never mentioned Andrew before. Had her daughter been making friends at school?

Daniel said, "I was surprised too, but it seems like Lyddie has made several friends. A few have been coming up to say *hello*."

"I'm so glad." Fern was thrilled her daughter seemed to be making friends. She wished she could stay and talk to Daniel, but she had work to do. She hurried back into the building.

Each time she came out, Daniel hurried over to her with a treat—funnel cakes, fry pies, soft pretzels.

"Stop," she said. "I know you love feeding people snacks." She laughed at his sheepish expression. He must have realized she was talking about the night he bought her cheese and crackers. "But I'm full."

"I want to be sure you stay warm." He walked beside her as she pushed Leroy, a new patient, to a display of wooden toys. Lowering his voice, he added, "And I want to spend more time with you." The message in his eyes as he looked at her made her heart flip over.

Leroy bought two toy trains, two wooden boats, three puzzles, a huge Noah's ark, and two dozen animals. "Thanks," he said to Fern. "My grandchildren will love the ark. We can keep that at our house. But we'll wrap the others for Christmas presents."

Daniel offered to carry the purchases back to the rehab center.

"What about Moses and Lyddie?"

He pointed to the picnic benches, where the two of them, with red cheeks and noses, had scrunched their wheelchairs close together at one end of a table. "They're eating pork barbecue and fries, so they should be all right until I get back."

At noontime, a woman pressed a steaming cup of chicken corn soup into her hand. "Pastor Martin asked me to give it to you," she said.

"*Danke*." Lydia was grateful for the warmth.

As usual, Daniel hurried over. "I'd been planning to get you some soup, but I see you already have some. *Daed* and Lyddie are chilly, so I'm going to take them inside to warm up. Then I can spend more time with you."

Fern's spirits soared. Daniel stayed with her as she brought other patients outside. All of them wanted raffle tickets, even if they didn't make any other purchases. And most of them bought food.

At quarter of two, Fern reached Margaret's room.

"I thought you'd never get here." Margaret could barely suppress her impatience to get outside. "I want that quilt they're auctioning at two."

Daniel stayed with them through the quilt auction. Margaret topped each bid as the price rose higher and higher. One hundred, two, two fifty.

"I'm freezing," Margaret whispered. The next time someone outbid her, she waved her number in the air and announced in a loud, quavering voice, "I bid four thousand dollars."

Fern gasped. She leaned over and whispered, "It's a gorgeous wedding ring quilt, but the price won't go much higher. Definitely not out of the hundreds."

"Four thousand. Going once, going twice." The auctioneer banged down his gavel. "Sold to the highest bidder."

Margaret patted Fern's hand. "Don't worry about it, dear. I have my reasons. Besides, it's for a worthy cause." Then she turned and winked at Daniel.

Still shaking her head, Fern pushed Margaret back to the rehab center while Daniel, clutching a handful of hundred-dollar bills, went to claim Margaret's quilt.

By the time, Fern had pushed three more people outside, the auction had ended, and vendors were packing up to leave. She took her last patient of the day up the ramp and into the building.

Darla rushed over to her, looking harried. "Could you do me a big favor? They're announcing the raffle winners in the auditorium, so we need to get everyone in there who'd like to attend."

All Fern wanted to do was kick off her shoes and collapse on one of the couches in the lobby for a few minutes to rest. Instead, the lobby was filled with bedlam. Sighing inwardly, she nodded. It was only fair for her to pitch in when the rest of the staff had done double duty inside while she pushed people around outside.

Ruthie rushed over. "Could we help bring in some patients?" She gestured to a crowd of children and parents from the schoolhouse.

"Why don't you ask Darla?" Fern suggested.

When Fern took Margaret into the auditorium, she was surprised to see Lyddie and Moses parked near the front of the room. Given a choice, her daughter always sat in the far corner in the back of the room. Moses, too, never came to events like this.

She didn't have time to wonder about it. People were pressing in on every side, and she still had more patients to bring in. She could barely squeeze the last few wheelchairs through the door.

The raffle prizes must be pretty special. Fern hadn't had a

chance to examine them closely, but from here they looked fairly average. She wished she could leave now, but she'd have to wait for Daniel.

He stood beside Lyddie, and when he caught sight of her, he beckoned to her. She debated staying where she was. It would be easier to get people out later, but he turned pleading eyes in her direction.

She wove her way through the crowd. When she finally made it to his side, he reached over and took her hand. Entwining his fingers through hers, he gave her a heart-stopping smile.

Fern's heart thumped so loudly she could barely hear Darla's announcement.

"Because it's so crowded in here," Darla said, "please just hold your winning ticket aloft and we'll tape the winning number to your item. You can claim your prize later." Then she announced the winning numbers to loud whistling and cheering.

Fern was glad when Darla pulled the final winning number. She couldn't wait to take everyone back to their rooms and go home to bed. It had been an exhausting day.

"Before everyone leaves," Darla said, "our money counters have been busy tallying up the take for today. We're grateful for all the vendors here today who donated generous shares of their profits."

A man scurried up to her and handed her a paper. When Darla read out the amount, the whole room burst into applause.

She held up her hand. "As many of you know, this fundraiser was organized by Daniel Graber." She pointed in his direction. "And he has a special announcement to make."

Daniel untangled his fingers from Fern's. Stunned, she stared at him as he walked up to stand beside Darla. Fern couldn't believe he'd done all this without her knowing.

He took the microphone Darla held out. "I'm grateful to all of you who participated in today's events. Thank you for your generosity." He paused for breath. "As you know, this fundraiser has a special purpose. To help one of your own rehab staff members, Fern Chupp, and your classmate, Lyddie. The money raised today will pay Lyddie's hospital bills."

Daniel pointed in their direction, and Fern froze as everyone turned to stare at them. Lyddie ducked her head. Moses reached out and laid a hand on Lyddie's shoulder.

As the crowd erupted into loud clapping and cheers, Daniel handed the microphone back to Darla and headed toward them. Fern stared at him, shocked, uncertain whether to rail at him for embarrassing them or thank him for his thoughtfulness.

She did neither. As Lyddie sometimes said, words got stuck in her mouth.

Daniel studied her, lines of anxiety on his forehead. "I hope you aren't upset with me." When she didn't answer, he said nervously, "I only wanted to help."

"Oh, Daniel. . ."

People around them moved toward the exits. She should offer to take people back to their rooms. Instead, she stood gazing into Daniel's eyes, her eyes misty.

"I wanted to help." He gestured to the audience behind them. "And so did they."

"I can't believe it," she whispered as tears started to fall.

❄

Daniel wished he could cradle her close and wipe away her tears. He couldn't tell if she was happy or upset. But he stayed lost in her eyes, trying to read the messages they were conveying.

All around them, people flocked toward the doors.

Daed cleared his throat loudly. "Why don't you two save that staring-into-each-other's-eyes stuff for some other time? Some of us would like to get back to our rooms. It's been a long day."

Breaking his gaze, Daniel focused on *Daed*. "I can take them both back, if you have things you need to do," Daniel offered.

Fern reached for the handles of Lyddie's wheelchair. "I'll take her first. Then I'd better see if anyone else needs help." Technically, she was off duty, but after all they'd done for her, it was the least she could do.

Daniel waited until she'd turned the wheelchair and headed out before he pivoted *Daed*'s and followed her. As soon as they reached *Daed*'s room, he helped his father into bed, and Fern pushed Lyddie's wheelchair close to him. Without saying a word, she rushed from the room.

Should he follow her or give her time alone?

"Go after her, son," *Daed* said. "And you'd better make things right with her because I'm not about to lose my chance to be with Lyddie." The last part of *Daed*'s sentence sounded like a threat.

Daniel had to talk to her, but he wasn't sure the busy hallway was the best setting. He paced up and down each corridor. No sign of Fern. He checked in the lobby and auditorium. Was she avoiding him?

Darla passed by with a young man in a wheelchair. He hurried after her.

"Do you know where Fern is?"

"Margaret asked Fern to take her back. She's in room twenty-two."

The door to Margaret's room was partially ajar. He debated about tapping, but decided he should wait. Margaret looked in his direction, and he ducked back so she couldn't see him.

"Come on in," Margaret called.

Evidently, he hadn't moved quickly enough. Embarrassed, he entered the room. Fern's eyes widened.

Margaret clapped her crooked, arthritic hands together. "How perfect." Then she turned to Fern. "The quilt, please?"

Fern laid the quilt across Margaret's lap. The older woman stroked the pinks and lavenders of the intertwining circles.

"Do you know what this pattern is?" she demanded.

"Double wedding ring." Fern's cheeks colored as Margaret pinned her with an intense gaze.

"Right." She turned to Daniel. "Do you know what circles symbolize, young man?" When he didn't answer, she said, "Circles have no end, so they mean eternity."

Daniel nodded.

"So here you have two circles linked for all eternity." She motioned for Fern to move around and stand by Daniel. "This is my wedding gift to the two of you."

"But—" Daniel started to say.

"We're not—" Fern said at the same time.

"Not yet." She handed the quilt to Fern, but she focused her attention on Daniel. "You'll know when the time is right."

Chapter Twelve

Lyddie's class practiced their Christmas program twice a day. So far, she'd never participated even though Ruthie tried to convince her to try. Lyddie had learned her part because *Mamm* tested her every night, and they sang the Christmas songs together.

The day of the program, Daniel picked her up after school, and she went straight to Moses's room as she always did. She slipped into his bathroom and put on the forest green dress *Mamm* had made. But she had a plan to escape. She was positive Moses would help her.

First, she made sure *Mamm* saw her in the dress—the one that matched her classmate's program clothes.

"Oh, Lyddie, you look lovely," *Mamm* said as she and Daniel peeked in the room. "I'll be done by seven, so I'll get in there just as the program starts. Be sure to meet Ruthie in the auditorium at six."

Lyddie didn't answer. She didn't want to lie. After *Mamm* left, she blew out a long, slow breath.

Down the hall, someone played Christmas carols on the piano in the auditorium. They didn't play instruments like the piano in

Lyddie's church, but it sounded pretty. She went to the door to listen.

"Close the door," Moses barked.

"You don't like music?"

"It hurts my ears." Moses lowered his head and mumbled into his beard. "And my heart."

"It makes you sad?"

He nodded. "This'll be a difficult Christmas." He sighed. "After almost sixty years together, this will be the first one without her."

Lyddie bit her lip. "And this will be my first Christmas without a grandpa."

"It's hard, isn't it?"

"*Jah*. Some mornings when I wake up, I think I'm going to see him. Then I open my eyes, and—" Tears clouded her view.

"I do that too." He gazed off into the distance. "I reach for her, but she's not there." Swallowing hard, he said, "I wanted a big family, but God had other plans. We only ever had one." A dry, choking noise came from his lips.

It sounded like he was trying to cry but didn't know how. Lyddie sat there silent and waited.

"Daniel has no family, so I have no grandchildren. I'm beginning to wonder if I ever will. With only the two of us, it'll be a lonely holiday."

His sad eyes made Lyddie want to comfort him. "If you want, you could pretend I'm your granddaughter," she offered shyly.

Moses's eyes shimmered with tears. "I'd like that."

When he opened his arms, and leaned over, Lyddie threw her arms around him and hugged him hard, almost tipping over her light wheelchair. The hug helped to fill the big *Dawdi*-sized hole inside.

This time Lyddie was the one who reached for the tissue box. She handed Moses a tissue. He turned his head away and wiped his eyes. Then he honked into the tissue.

"Don't you have to be somewhere at six o'clock?" he asked in a gruff voice and pointed at the clock.

The program. Lyddie had forgotten all about it. And her plan.

"You know how you don't like music?" Her lower lip trembled. If he didn't agree, she'd have to perform. "I don't either. At least not when I have to do it in front of people."

"You're supposed to sing in the auditorium with your class?"

Lyddie ducked her head. "*Jah,* but I'm too scared. And I don't like people staring at me." She made circles on the chair arm with her fingertip. "Besides, what if I forget my poem?"

"You're supposed to recite a poem too?"

She nodded.

"Will you recite it for me?"

"I guess." Lyddie hoped her unenthusiastic answer would make him change his mind, but Moses's face brightened. She said her piece.

He looked thoughtful. "I don't enjoy being in crowds like that, but I would like to hear your poem. I'd always hoped to listen to my grandchildren perform in school programs someday."

She'd promised to be his pretend granddaughter. If she did this, she'd make him happy, but her throat closed up at the thought.

"Please, Lyddie?"

Moses had never said *please* to her before. And he was sad. She wanted to cheer him up.

She pushed the words past her tight throat muscles. "All right."

He pushed the bell to call for help, and Lyddie prayed it wouldn't be *Mamm*. Martha came in and helped Moses into the wheelchair. Lyddie followed behind as Martha took Moses to the auditorium. He asked her to put them on the far side of the room where it was darker.

At the front of the room, stood a huge Christmas tree with blinking lights. Is that what angels looked like all shiny and bright? *Mamm* only decorated with a few pine branches on the mantel, so Lyddie stared, fascinated by the glitter.

Until she realized that, beside the tree, everyone in her class had already assembled for the program. They stood behind Darla who was giving a welcoming speech.

"It's too late," Lyddie whispered, relieved not to have to perform.

"No, it's not," Moses whispered back. "They haven't started yet."

Lyddie shrank closer to his wheelchair. "I can't go up there in front of all these people." She clutched his armrest so tightly, the padding hissed out air.

Moses pointed to the grand piano beside the group of students. "If you sneak along the wall there, you could circle around the piano without anyone noticing. You'd come out right behind that boy on the end. Isn't that Andrew?"

Lyddie turned terrified eyes toward Moses to see if he was serious. He was. His eyes shone with confidence that she could do it. Her stomach warned her she couldn't.

"Please? For me?" Moses asked.

As she stared into his eyes and read the message he was sending, Lyddie wanted to shake her head, tell him *no*. But how could she refuse?

"But. I'm. scared." Her words came out choppy and uncertain.

"You can do it, Lyddie. I believe in you."

Darla reached the end of her speech and introduced Ruthie. If Lyddie didn't go now, she'd be too late.

With one last glance at Moses's pleading eyes, Lyddie took a deep breath.

I believe in you echoed over and over in her head. The words rose and fell in time to the terrible waves crashing in her stomach.

Head down, she edged her wheelchair along the wall. Nobody seemed to notice. They were all listening to Ruthie talk about the school and the student project.

When the piano hid her from the audience, Lyddie stopped. She could stay here until the program was over. No one would know. No one except Moses.

Moses who'd said, *I believe in you.*

He wanted to see her perform. Lyddie forced herself to wheel her chair the last few feet.

Andrew blocked her from view. Maybe this wouldn't be so bad after all. She couldn't see the audience, and they couldn't see her.

Ruthie finished talking and turned to the students. Her eyebrows rose when she spied Lyddie. Then her lips widened into a huge, welcoming smile. She motioned for the scholars closest to her to move over to make more room for Lyddie.

When they did, Lyddie faced a sea of heads and eyes, all looking in her direction. Her stomach whirled. She felt dizzy. What if she fainted? Would she fall face-forward out of the wheelchair? She wanted to rush around the piano, race down the hall and into Moses's room, and slam the door.

But Ruthie started speaking, and everyone turned toward her. Everyone except Lyddie. She sought out Moses in the back corner. His huge smile became her anchor. If she kept eye contact with him, the ocean of people around her disappeared. The waves of panic still rose and fell in her stomach, but Moses kept her from drowning.

Ruthie motioned for them to start the first song, but fear had cut off Lyddie's breath. She'd never be able to sing. She opened her mouth, but no notes came out.

She mouthed the words until her voice caught up. When the song ended, she wanted to look for *Mamm*, but if she took her eyes off Moses, she'd sink.

One by one, the others recited poems or did skits. The closer it came to Lyddie's turn, the waves in her stomach splashed into the back of her throat and burned going down.

When Ruthie called Lyddie's name, she squeezed her eyes shut and wished she could disappear. All the words to her poem scattered and floated around in her head. How did it start? She couldn't remember.

The silence as everyone waited made the words spin faster. Then Moses's face appeared before her. She was doing this for him. She pretended she was in his room. She took a deep breath and said the words to him again.

When everyone clapped, Lyddie opened her eyes. Moses had the biggest smile she'd ever seen. She sang the final song as loudly as she could—just for him.

When Darla stood up to announce upcoming programs, Lyddie slunk around the big piano and wheeled herself back to where Moses was sitting.

"You sang like an angel," Moses said in a choked voice.

"That's because I was singing for *Dawdi* and you."

His big callused hand closed over hers in a gentle squeeze.

❄

Daniel nudged Fern and motioned toward *Daed* and Lyddie. "Look at the two of them."

Her eyes misty, Fern watched Moses take Lyddie's hand. "I'm grateful your *daed* has been so kind to her. She's been missing her *dawdi*." Her voice broke. "This will be our first Christmas without him."

"I'm so sorry. I know how hard that can be." Daniel reached for her hand to comfort her.

"Lyddie's shyness has always kept her from making friends, so she counted on *Dawdi* to listen." Fern sucked in a shaky breath. "We never would have made it without him after my husband died. *Dawdi* was Lyddie's rock. Mine too. It's been hard on her not to have a father figure."

Daniel could think of someone who'd love to be that father figure.

"That's why I'm so grateful she has your *daed*," Fern continued in a tear-choked voice.

Daed could stand in for Lyddie's *dawdi*. But Daniel wanted to be Lyddie's *daed*. If Fern would agree.

Margaret had said he'd know when the time was right. But he couldn't ask her here in this crowded room. He drew her into the doorway of the darkened room next door.

But once they were alone, his throat tightened. What if she said *no*? He'd never know until he asked.

"Daniel?" She said in a soft, breathy voice, glancing up at him.

He got lost in the beauty and depth of her eyes. "Fern?" he managed to say.

Her quiet *jah?* set his pulse tripping until he realized it wasn't an answer to the question burning in his heart. "If we were younger, I'd ask to court you."

She lowered her eyelids, but the light in her eyes had already died.

He plunged on, "But we've had time to get to know each other here, and I know you're the woman I love and would like to marry. Would you—"

Fern took a step back, and Daniel's spirits plunged. He hadn't even finished the question. He steeled himself for her rejection.

"I don't know what to say."

Then don't say anything at all, Daniel begged her silently. *Let's go back to being friends.*

"This is hard for me." She pleated the fabric of her apron with nervous fingers. "You see. . ."

If only he could erase what he'd said, blot it out and start over. "Listen, you don't have to—" he stuttered. "I should never—"

Fern interrupted him. "I have a confession."

No, please don't tell me you're planning to marry someone else.

"I vowed I could never bear to lose anyone I loved. It was easier not to let my heart get entangled. I-I was attracted to you from the first time we met, but. . ." She drew in a shuddery breath.

"But you can't love me."

She gazed up at him with wide, startled eyes. "No, no. Ever since then, I've been fighting not to fall in love with you. But my heart refused to listen."

"You mean—"

"I love you. But I'm so scared I'll lose you."

Daniel wrapped his arms around her and drew her close. "There's no way I can guarantee the future, but we do have the present."

"To answer your question. . ."

"But I didn't get to ask it yet."

Her slow, gentle smile heated him from head to toe. "That's all right. I already know what it is. And the answer is *jah*."

"In that case. . ." He backed up until they were under the mistletoe. "Do you know what this means?"

She giggled, but then his lips met hers. She twined her arms around his neck, and he pulled her closer as the kiss deepened.

❄

Moses cleared his throat. "Well, well, well."

Lyddie twisted her head around to see what he was looking at.

In a dark corner of the room, Daniel had his arms around *Mamm*.

"I'm thinking you won't have to be my pretend granddaughter for long. You'll be my real one." He leaned over and put an arm around her to give her a squeeze. "And I bet I'll soon have lots of grandchildren."

"Do you think so?" Lyddie bounced in her chair, bubbling over with excitement. Being an only child was lonely. She'd always wished for brothers and sisters. Now her wish might come true.

Moses winked at her. "I'm positive."

Lyddie grinned at him. Her whole insides sparkled like the twinkling lights on the Christmas tree. God had given them all a special family for Christmas. And, in addition to Jesus, that was the very best gift of all.

About the Author

Inspirational author Rachel J. Good writes life-changing, heart-tugging novels of faith, hope, and forgiveness. She is the author of several Amish series in print or forthcoming – *Sisters & Friends* series, *Love & Promises* series, and two books in the *Hearts of Amish Country* series – as well as the *Amish Quilts Coloring Books* and the contemporary novella, *Angels Unaware*, part of the *Hope Chapel* series. Rachel also juggles freelance editing and illustration careers. She loves reading (of course!), traveling, and spending time with her five children and three grandchildren. Visit her at her website, Facebook, author page, Twitter, Pinterest, and Goodreads.

Enjoyed Love's Christmas Blessings?

Check out these other Amish Collections from Celebrate Lit Publishing

Spring of Love

Love's Thankful Heart

Plain Everyday Heroes

Made in the USA
Monee, IL
18 May 2020

31336703R00139